The Tale of Amon
Book Two

by Jeff Reedy

The Tales of Elidria: Book Two

Dallas, Texas

Preface

Welcome back! Once again, I'm very excited to be sharing this journey with you. It's an odd and wonderful closeness that I feel with you, the reader. Not just because you chose to read my book, but you read the first one and came back for more!

And you probably remember the caveats that I gave at the beginning of the last book. That the book was very dialog driven and short on descriptors. In this book, you will find something new. While there is still a lot of dialog, there is more description now. And one HUGE change that you'll find is that the first book was almost entirely about Amon and Amy. You probably remember that there were a few other characters, but most of the book was about those two. Well, you're about to meet many new characters! This is exciting to me, because I love these characters, and I think you will, too.

One thing that might bother you in this second book is that there are MANY chapters, and the chapters are very short. The story jumps back and forth between several different plotlines. Once you get used to it, I think you might enjoy it. But if not, let me know, and I'll try to reduce the number of breaks and chapters in both subsequent books and even in the second edition of this one. Isn't that cool? You get to participate in how the story is told. I'll just go back in time and fix it. ☺

Anyway, without further ado, please enjoy Book Two of the Tale of Amon.

jeff

Tale of Amon: Book Two

Amon stood in a very strange room. The floor was a dark red fluid that flowed slowly across the room. The walls were mirrors, and the ceiling seemed to be some kind of stone, black but flat, not glossy. It was about a hundred feet above his head, Amon guessed.

In the center of the room was a reclined chair, reminding Amon of a dentist's chair. Around the chair were dozens of things that looked like windows, but each one showed something different. A young Asian woman was in the chair, looking at all of the windows. Amon stood next to her, and Amy was talking with Dorian nearby.

Dorian excused himself. "I'm sorry, Amon. I've got an important message coming in, I need to take it."

Amy glanced at Dorian. "Do you need me?"

"I don't think so, not right now. It's Isha."

"Oh, OK. Let me know."

And Dorian was gone.

"Seems like a good guy," observed Amon.

"He's the best. Always there for you when you need somebody. He's a great leader, and gets put into tough situations pretty often. But he's good at taking care of the group."

"He's not the leader you told me about?"

"No. We'll talk about him later. He's gone missing."

"What is this room? What is she doing?" he spoke in a hushed voice. He could tell the woman in the chair was doing something interesting and important.

"She's monitoring," said Amy. "That means she's looking at the information that's coming from all of those video cameras I told you about, that we've put all over the place. She's looking to see if anyone needs help. She's also collecting info on what the bad guys are doing."

"The DaiUi?"

"Among others."

An ancient looking African man came into the room. "Greetings, Amy. Is this Amon?"

Amy nodded. "Amon, this is Tembo."

The old man looked at Amon intently, "Tell me, Amon. How did you get here?" Tembo had a strong African accent.

"Well... I used to be a crewman on a Nazi sub. I felt ... like we were doing wrong things. That we were killing good people. One day this girl... well, you know Amy... she showed up on the sub. Just appeared out of nowhere. She told me about you guys. She invited me to join you. Then all of these people showed up, trying to kill me. Amy protected me from them. One woman even... even ate some of the other crewmen. But Amy didn't let any of them hurt me. Then we pulled this decoy trick, and the other immortal bad guys fell for it, and she ... Amy dropped me off in Germany and let me think about it. I decided to join you, and so she flew me to Florida and ... and took me into the fountain and did the thing with the dagger. Then I woke up here, in Sri Kaǎsala." Amon finished and looked at the old man curiously.

There was a long pause. Then the old man said, "Thank you for telling me that delightful story. What I actually meant was, did you come into this room from the discussion room? Because I was wondering if Serena was in there."

The old man laughed. Amy's eyes glittered. A tiny smile turned the corner of the lips of the woman in the chair. The old man laughed as only men from Africa can, with joyful abandon and white shining teeth, head thrown back and voice filling the room.

"No, I haven't been in there yet," Amon smiled amiably.

"Well, then. Let me excuse myself. There is something important happening that I need to talk to her about. I'll catch up with you later?" his eyes asked for forgiveness.

"Of course! I look forward to it."

Tembo left. Amon turned to Amy with a sheepish grin.

"OK. So what's next?"

"Now, you get to meet Sri Kaǎsala and the people who live here."

"That sounds exciting."

"It is. Just wait."

They walked across the floor of the flowing red fluid. It solidified under each of their steps. Amon was fascinated. He looked at the fluid under his feet, stepping more slowly with each step as they crossed to the door. They went down the hall, which was white, with paintings every few feet on both sides. It looked like a hallway in an art museum. "Do you guys collect art? Like... from different times?"

"No, we leave art where we find it. Or sometimes we take it to museums. But all of the art in Sri Kaǎsala is by the Ui."

"This looks like Picasso's Guernica. And this has to be a Rembrandt."

"They were painted in those styles. The one that looks like Guernica is actually a retelling of a terrible slaughter that happens in Delphi in 2097."

"Didn't the oracle warn people?"

"Yes, but they never listen."

"What about the Rembrandt?"

"It's a portrait of that leader I was telling you about. The one who was Sphered."

"So is Sphering someone killing them?"

"No. It's easier to show you than to tell you what Sphering is. We'll demonstrate it for you when you meet more of us."

They continued down the hall. "These are amazing," said Amon. "Some of the styles I don't recognize, though. Like this one, with the ephemeral haziness interspersed with these translucent geometric designs? It has a faint feel of maybe Salvador Dali, but there are aspects I don't recognize."

"You are surprisingly well informed about art for a Nazi sub crewman."

"Ja, most of my fellow soldiers didn't share my passion for art."

"Speaking of passions, are you ready to start learning other languages?"

"Ja! I love learning things."

"I can tell. So what language do you want to learn next?"

"What language do you guys usually speak here?"

"We alternate between English and the Ancient Tongue."

"Why English?"

"Because about one hundred years after you were born, it starts becoming the standard world language on Earth. And within fifty years, everyone on Earth speaks it fluently."

"Wow. Why? What happens to German and French and Chinese and all of the other languages?"

"There are still people who speak them, as a second language. But everyone speaks English because the world becomes so small that a common language is needed, and English wins the fight."

"The world becomes small?"

"Yeah, technology makes it so that everyone can talk to everybody all of the time. It doesn't matter where you are, you can instantly have a conversation with anyone else on the planet. And English got the upper hand along the way, so it just nudged everyone else out."

"English it is, then."

"One good way to learn English, once you get the basics down, is to watch movies and TV shows."

"If you say so."

"It helps you to learn pronunciation and idioms better than anything you can do in the classroom. So we'll give you a few basic lessons and then let you watch a bunch of movies."

"By 'a few' and 'a bunch' I'm guessing you mean hundreds and thousands?"

"You're catching on quick."

Amon was startled by his feelings. "Wow," he said.

"What?"

"Well…. I've always been a curious kind of guy. I really enjoy learning new things. But just now… my desire to learn was so strong it was almost painful. It's like I can't WAIT to get started learning English…"

"Oh, yeah. That makes sense. When you're one of us, all of your senses and desires are heightened, but especially the ones that are already strong in your mind naturally."

"That's interesting. And it reminds me. You said when we were on the sub that you were older, stronger, and smarter than I was. I know you're still older than I am, but are you still stronger and smarter?"

"Well, do you want to find out?"

Amon was startled. "Um. Sure. How?"

"Let's arm wrestle."

They were still walking down the hallway. Amon laughed. "OK… where?"

Amy led him into a gigantic room filled with couches, tables, and chairs. The floors were polished marble, so clean and smooth that he could see the furniture reflected in it. The walls were a dark blue hue, but as he moved into the room, they seemed to change. A light in the wall rose to his left, swept through the walls around the room clockwise, and then vanished into the floor on his right. A breeze blew through the room, bringing the scent of freshly cut grass.

Amy led him to two chairs with a table between them. She sat down in one and put her elbow on the table in classic arm-wrestling pose. There were a couple dozen people in the room already, and one of them, a mountain of a man with long blond hair, came over with a smile and watched the challenge.

"Is this the famous Amon?" the huge man asked. He was wearing brown pants of some tough, thick material Amon hadn't seen before, a dark gray sweater, and black boots. His hair was an enormous dark blond tangle down his back. He was probably over seven feet tall, from Amon's estimation, and looked like he weighed around 400 pounds, all muscle.

Amon sat down across from Amy and put his elbow on the table. She grabbed his hand. The big man grinned even bigger.

Amy nodded, "Amon, Eric. Eric, Amon."

Eric laughed and clapped Amon on the back. He fell forward under the blow. It was a friendly greeting, but it felt like being welcomed by a thunderstorm.

"OK," said Amy. "Are you ready?"

"Did he ask how strong you are?" asked Eric.

"Something like that."

"I... think so," said Amon.

"Go," said Eric.

Amon put everything he had into it. He was a strong guy. The tendons stood out on his arm, and he leaned with his whole body. Amy's hand kept his hand straight up, not moving an inch.

"It's... like.... wrestling... a statue..." gasped Amon.

A few more people came closer to watch. They didn't gather around them, but gave them room to breathe.

The clasped hands moved very slightly, showing that Amy was starting to win.

"Are you ... letting me... struggle?" asked Amon.

"I want you to feel like you're doing well," said Amy. She sounded casual, like she wasn't even trying. "Do you want to use both hands?"

Amon looked incredulous. Then he grabbed the clasped hands with his other hand and pulled with all of his strength. The clasped hands stayed exactly where they were. Then they moved another inch toward Amy's victory.

Amy suddenly got her far-away look. She quickly beat Amon, not exactly slamming his hands down, but very quickly pushing them against the table, and then said, "We need to talk to Dorian. Something happened."

Amon tried to recover from being tossed aside like a rag. Eric was quicker at responding. "What's up?"

"Strode, Isha, and Serena went to rescue the Atachis," Amy started.

"Yeah, I guess they can reveal that they're not really Amon and you now, right?"

"They can without putting Amon at risk. But they are still in danger of staying Sphered if they do."

They got up and left the table, going to some couches nearby. Dorian came into the room then and joined them.

"So what's the latest?" asked Amy. She, Eric, and Dorian sat on the couch. Amon recovered and came over to join them. A couple other Ui nearby came and sat on nearby couches, taking in the discussion.

"Serena, Alisha, and Strode were able to spring the Atachis. Serena, Strode, and the Atachis are on their way back here," said Dorian.

"What about Isha?" Amy asked.

"Alisha stayed there. She told Serena and Strode she was going to try to get some help from them regarding the Miramar situation. But Serena noticed that Damien was there, as well."

"Oh, no," Amy looked distressed.

"Is that bad?" asked Amon.

"Isha and Damien have history," said Amy.

"And even though she's in a relationship here, she still struggles with feelings for Damien," put in Eric. It was funny hearing such a sensitive statement coming from the enormous man.

"So she's ... where? With the enemy?" asked Amon.

"Yes, but the lines get blurry when you are talking about Isha and the enemy."

"Oh... she's.... does she..."

"No," said Dorian. "She's one of us. But she has relationships with many of them. And she tries to build bridges. It doesn't always work out."

Amon digested this. Then he noticed something.

"Hey... I'm not hungry."

Eric laughed. "Not sure I've heard someone say they're NOT hungry as an announcement before... but while you're at it, I'm not sleepy!"

Amon chuckled. "Ja, I guess that's an unusual thing to say. And by the way, thanks for speaking German, everyone."

"Oh, we're not," explained Amy. "We're speaking a mix of English and the Ancient Tongue. But when you were Changed, that layer of molecules I told you about? The tiny little computers? They are on your eardrums now. Until you learn English and the Ancient Tongue, you will have everything translated into German by that layer. Of course, we do all understand German, so when you reply, we hear you speaking German."

"Wow. That's... amazing."

"And very handy," mentioned Eric. He was sipping something from an enormous stein.

Dorian looked like he was staring into space, but Amon had seen this look before. Even though Dorian was sitting on the couch nearby, Amon knew he was interacting with people all over the place… maybe all over the universe?

"I think the best thing for you to do right now," thought Amy out loud, "is to watch some movies and shows. It'll get you caught up on a lot of things… language, cultural references, and jokes. We'll be able to talk more naturally with you once you have a shared frame of reference."

"Won't that take a long time?"

"Well, you'll get used to this after a while… but that doesn't matter here. Time is different here than you're used to. You could go watch movies for two thousand years, and it would feel like an hour. You wouldn't get tired, or bored…"

"Or hungry," put in Amon.

"Oh yeah. That's where we started this conversation. You're not hungry?"

"At all. And it's been… hours? Since I ate last?"

"It's been two weeks since you ate last."

Amon's mouth fell open. "How… is that … possible?"

"You're immortal now. That means you don't have to eat, drink, sleep, or even breathe anymore. You don't NEED to do anything. Anything you do from now on will be because you choose to, not because you need to."

"So you can get a snack if you want. But only if you feel like eating. Otherwise don't worry about it. You never have to eat again."

"How does that work? Where does my energy come from?"

"We'll explain that later. For now, let's get you settled in, watching some shows. Do you want popcorn?"

".... Sure? Is that a thing?"

"Yes. For decades, people ate popcorn while watching movies. It's a tradition."

"OK. Where do I go?"

"We have a room for that. It's not like a movie theater, because you don't need one. You can watch a movie right here. But it keeps you from being distracted by other people, and it also prevents you from feeling self-conscious while you're sitting there watching movies."

Amon followed Amy out of the discussion room and back into the hallway. They went down the hall toward the fountain room, and Amon marveled at the artwork again. They went past the fountain room and came to a room filled with recliners. There was an alcove in the wall with a small box in it that looked kind of like a washing machine. Amy went to it, tapped on the lid, and then opened the top and took out a bag of popcorn.

"You lock up the popcorn in there?"

Amy's eyes danced. "No. That's a 3D printer."

"A ... what?"

"It's a device that makes whatever you want. If you want a lamp, you type in what kind you want and it makes it. If you want a bag of popcorn, you type that in, and it makes popcorn. Anything you want."

"Can it make a person?"

"It can make a body. But not a live one."

"Why would you want to make a dead body?"

Amy shot a look at him. "I didn't say we did. But we do, actually. It's excellent for when we are learning medicine."

"Oh, some of you are doctors?"

"All of us are doctors."

"Oh yeah. I keep forgetting the whole 'forever' thing."

"So you can't make a living person?"

"Yes and no."

"I'm beginning to think that's your answer for everything."

"Not everything. But most things."

"So how is it yes and no this time? It seems like you could either make a living person or you can't."

"Well, this gets into what I was telling you about computers."

"Adding machines are people, too?" Amon looked at Amy. "What? Your eyes are doing that thing again."

"You made another joke."

"I did?"

"You make the best jokes without meaning to."

"What did I say this time?"

"There is a meme where-"

"A what? A meme?"

"Yes. It's… it's a theme that you keep repeating, but with different things subbed in. There's a meme where you say 'dogs are people, too' or 'kids are people, too'. You just said 'computers are people, too.'"

"Actually I said adding machines."

"Yeah, but you were talking about computers. And yes, they ARE people, too. And we can make them."

"So you can make people."

"Yes and no."

"So how is it no?"

"Well, it gets very complicated in saying how it's not. Because we can 3D print a human body with fully functional organs. And then we can place a sentient computer into that functioning human body. So in a sense, it's a human being. But in another sense, it's … an adding machine, as you would say. It's an incredibly complex computer that gives every indication that it is self-aware and a person."

"So how do you know it's not?"

"We don't. Hence the confusion…. And the blurred line. We CAN make a being that claims to be sentient and is made out of human organs. We don't know for certain if it's actually sentient and a person, or if it's just a glorified adding machine that pretends to be a person."

"How can you find out?"

"In a sense, we never can. We can ask them, but they just say that they ARE self-aware and a person. But that's what they would say whether it was true or not. So we treat them like human beings… we err on the side of respecting their dignity."

"So maybe you can make people and maybe you can't?"

"Exactly: yes and no. We can make creatures that claim to be persons. We can't make human beings."

"Except the old-fashioned way?" asked Amon.

"That's always an option."

"So you guys… some of you…"

"Not often. Like I told you earlier, some of us do get married. And a few of us that get married have children. But it's an even bigger commitment than marriage, right? Because-"

"Because the child is immortal, too?"

"Yes."

"But…. When you become immortal, don't you stop aging?"

"Yes."

"So how does… how can you have a baby that is born and grows up… if it never ages?"

"The child can choose to grow up."

"Really grow up? Or just appear to?"

"How do you mean that?"

"Well, you appear to be ten. But you're actually millions of years old. But if you chose to, you could look twenty. Or forty. Or a hundred."

"I see. So you're asking if the baby can choose to really grow up like a normal person, or just appear however they want?"

"Yes."

"What's the difference?"

Amon thought about it. "I'm not sure." He thought for a while. "But... how does it... when it's still in the womb? Does it... mature?"

"Yes, the baby grows up. But its growth isn't preset. As soon as it is old enough, it can take over control of its growth. It can go back. It can stop."

"How old is old enough?"

"It's different for different people. Some of them take control at three. Some can't control it until they're five. We had one take control at eighteen months."

"Do any of them stay ... toddlers?"

"No. So far everyone has decided to at least reach the age of ten."

Amon looked at Amy pointedly.

"That's not my story. I was changed when I was ten."

"So this is kind of like a –" he stopped midsentence.

"A what?" asked Amy.

"I'm sorry. I don't want to..."

"It's OK. You won't learn if you censor your questions."

"Well, it just seems like... with you and the cool kids... never growing up... it's like a real-life Peter Pan and the lost kids..."

"You're right. It's like we're in Neverland."

"Is there a Captain Hook?"

"Lots of them."

"Are they all mad about alligators?"

"Crocodiles. And no."

Amon started to ask another question. Amy stopped him. "You are a never-ending stream of questions. And that's good. You will learn really well that way. But right now, you should watch these movies and shows and get caught up on cultural references."

"How many am I watching?"

"Thousands."

Amon settled in and pushed play.

Amy went back to her quarters, picked up a Sphere, and whispered to it.

Chapter Two

Amon finished a movie and turned off his viewer. He stretched. He felt like he'd watched about a three-hour movie. But he suspected he'd watched a lot more than that.

He got up and went into the hallway. He felt like he was probably looking for Amy, but he wasn't sure. He wandered down the hall until a painting caught his attention. It looked like a Jackson Pollock. But there was something about it that he couldn't quite figure out.

The style was Pollock, but there was a theme… or tone… or mood… or something that was just beneath the surface of his conscious thought. There was a vibrancy… a power… just under the obvious swirls and drips of paint.

He stood for a few minutes, pondering the depths of the paint on the canvas when he heard a woman's voice say from behind him, "Do you like it?"

"It's powerful," said Amon. "I can't figure out what it is… but there's something deeply stirring about it."

"How does it make you feel?"

Amon turned and looked at the woman. She was about 5'11", with long dark brown hair. Her hair had streaks of light brown in it. Her complexion was dark, and she was exotic in a way that he couldn't quite place. She was wearing gray slacks, a sweater that was the color blue he had only seen in paintings of Mary, and the ubiquitous black boots.

"Well, the surface is calm and peaceful. It makes me feel serene. But under that calm surface, I sense something powerful. I don't know what to call it, but it won't let go."

A smile played at the corners of the woman's mouth. "You're pretty perceptive."

"Oh. Thanks. I'm Amon, by the way."

"Yeah… we've been waiting for you."

Amon laughed. "That would sound creepy coming from most people. But you make it sound somehow profound. Why does everyone keep saying that? Is there something I'm going to do?"

"Yes."

Amon waited. He was trying to pull an Amy.

The woman also waited in comfortable silence. Amon put out his hand to shake hers. She took his hand between both of hers and held it, not shaking it, just looking into his eyes. Amon was never sure what to do when the Ui would do this, but he sensed that he didn't have to do anything. Just be.

He sensed something happening in the woman's face, but he wasn't sure how he was perceiving this, since her face didn't change.

"What's your name?" he asked.

"I'm Serena."

Chapter Three

Amy finished whispering to her Sphere and put it back in its setting. She hopped up off her bed and went down the hall. She navigated the maze of hallways that could get even the best explorer lost in Sri Kaǎsala, and then came down the hall where Amon and Serena were talking.

"Did Serena explain her painting to you?" she asked Amon.

"YOU painted this??" he turned to Serena. Serena nodded, shooting a look at Amy.

"Did you not… want me to know that?" asked Amon, sounding confused.

"I was going to see if you could guess," Serena explained, appearing disappointed.

"Don't worry. He'll have plenty more to guess," pointed out Amy.

"Where did you go?" asked Amon. "I was going to ask you how many movies I watched…"

"Did you lose count?"

"I wasn't counting…"

Serena smiled. "Don't let her make you feel guilty. You weren't supposed to count."

"You watched 7,342 movies and 627 TV shows," said Amy.

"Episodes?"

"Series."

"Wow," said Amon. "I was in there a long time."

"Not really. You were in there two days."

"How did…" he trailed off. Amy, Serena, and Amon walked into the discussion room and sat down.

"You can watch things much faster than you used to. You could watch all of the movies and shows known to man in less than a week."

"Well, I could do that before, too. I just wouldn't get any of it."

"Now you get all of it. You can recall every episode you've seen. You know every line. It's all in your active memory."

"How is that possible? It seems like I would… run out of room?"

"Well, the human brain is capable of remembering a vast amount of information, even before enhancement. But your brain has been enhanced."

"It has? When did that happen?"

"In the fountain. When you were changed. You can remember everything now."

"I don't feel like I can."

"You need to be trained."

"When does that start?"

"Some of it has started already. But the majority of it will take place over the next few centuries."

Amon nodded. Then he smiled. "That sounds crazy."

"That it takes so long?"

"I still haven't gotten used to forever. Taking centuries just to

LEARN something. It's mind boggling."

"Well, if you grasped it this fast, you'd be setting a record."

"How long does it usually take?"

"At least a few years."

"I need to go monitor," said Serena.

"OK, catch up with you later. Are the Atachis back yet?"

"No, but they're on their way."

"Ping me when you find out where they are, would you?"

"Sure. Need me to tell them anything?"

"No, I just wanted to talk to them. It's not a formal thing."

"Got it. I'll ping."

Serena left.

"She's going to… monitor?"

"Yes. Remember when I told you we have cameras set up all through time?"

"Vaguely."

"Well, someone has to monitor them and keep an eye out for what's happening out there."

"And she does that?"

"She's very good at it."

Amon was quiet for a few beats. This troubled Amy, since he hadn't shut up since she met him.

"You OK?"

"Well, thinking about Serena monitoring made me think of all the life I'm leaving behind."

"You said you weren't close to your family, right?"

"Ja. I'm not. But my friends from home, my car, all of the places that were home to me. I … guess I've started missing them."

"Well, I've got a surprise for you."

"Ja? What kind of surprise?"

Amy held up a small black rock. It was so black that it made Amon's eyes hurt a little, and his mind did strange things when he looked at it.

"That's REALLY black…" he said.

"Yeah, it's blacker than vantablack."

"What's that?"

"Well, vantablack was developed in the 21st century. It's made of tiny little tubes that are smaller than you can see, and they absorb 99.8% of all light. But this material is blacker than that. It absorbs so close to 100% that the difference is outside of human detection. In essence, it absorbs all light that hits it."

"So that's why it looks weird?"

"Yes. Think about it. If it's absorbing all light, then you can't really see it. Any light that would normally bounce off of it and come to your eyes is absorbed instead. You're actually just seeing where the Memory Stone WOULD be. You're not really seeing it."

"It's a Memory Stone? To help me remember something?"

"No, it's like… well, it's a memory storage device. It's hard to explain because you don't really know computers."

"It's like a floppy disk? Or a CD?"

"Oh yeah. I forgot you just watched a bajillion movies. You're familiar now."

Amon smiled. "I'm all caught up."

"Yes, it's like that. But it also interacts with you."

"How?"

"OK, just to prepare you, this is going to be weird."

Amon looked like he was steeling himself.

"So I want you, in a few seconds, to look at the stone again. But when you do, you're going to feel like you're being transported to another place. It's OK. You'll still be here with me. Trust me again."

"OK."

Amy nodded. "OK, look at the stone."

Amon looked.

Chapter Four

Amy said it was going to be weird, but Amon was not ready for this. He looked at the stone, and suddenly he was not in the room with Amy anymore. He was standing in some grass behind a building. The sun was shining, and it was cool outside. He looked around. It looked vaguely familiar. He had been here before.

He walked around the building and saw that it was the shed behind his house in Germany. He saw the cows in the nearby pasture. He saw his black Volkswagen Beetle sitting in front of his house. He walked over to it, a little faster than he intended, and ran his hand along the roof. It felt real. He looked inside and saw the dent in the dashboard where his sister had tossed him a hatchet once and he dropped it. It was a tiny dent, but it was there. The tiny little red dot was on the steering wheel.

He raised his head and looked around. Everything was exactly as he remembered it. He saw the farmer who lived next door and owned the cows puttering around his barn, and he could faintly make out the sounds of the old man muttering to himself like he always did.

Suddenly Amy came around the side of the shed where he had just come from.

"Does this look familiar?" she asked.

"It's my home. Exactly as I remember it."

She nodded. "I'll explain how it works, but first, it's important for me to teach you how to get back. Go like this…" she flicked her thumb against her other fingers of the same hand, like she was pretending to light a cigarette lighter, and her thumb would be the pretend flame.

Amon did it, too. He saw a green flame flickering on the tip of his thumb. It didn't burn him. He couldn't feel it. But he could see it.

"That's how you know you're here."

"How I know I'm… where?" asked Amon, looking around his German yard.

"That rock you looked at… it's called a Memory Stone. When it's activated and you look at it, it interacts with the nerve synapses in your visual cortex. In simple terms, it interfaces with your brain through your eyes."

"That sounds painful."

"Did it hurt?"

"…. No."

"It's pretty advanced tech. So the bugs have all been worked out. It doesn't hurt at all. But what it does do is it reads the memories in your brain and then allows you to enter those memories."

"And you're still trying to tell me this isn't magic."

"Not even a little magic."

"So how are you here?"

"I'm interacting with your memory, too. You can also interact with people you remember. They will be what we jokingly call NPC's most of the time. Though people can control them if you want…"

"You lost me."

"OK, see that farmer over there?"

Amon nodded and looked at the muttering farmer.

"Right now, no one is controlling that … well, we'll call him a character. So he's not real. If you went over and shot him, no one would die. You would just be turning off a video game character."

"OK, I see. But what were you saying about someone I know?"

"Well, right now I'm interacting with you as me. I figured that would be less confusing. But watch...." Amy vanished. Then the farmer suddenly looked at Amon and walked over to the fence.

"See? Now I'm the farmer," said the farmer.

"... Is that you, Amy?"

"Yes. I'm just controlling the farmer character in your memory."

"Why would .... I want that? Like, I mean, why would the person with the memory want someone to control one of their... characters?"

"Various reasons. It can be fun. I won't go into all of the reasons, because some are kind of personal. But some people really like to relive their memories, and they like to share those memories with friends. It can be interesting to do it with the friend controlling another character, or it can be fun when they're separate, like this...."

The farmer walked away and Amy reappeared beside Amon.

"This... is really strange."

"You can go other places, too. Right now, you're just in your head. Like, you're not controlling a physical person. Your body is just standing there back at Śri Kaāsala. Nothing in the physical world is moving based on your thoughts. But you can do that, too."

"Do what?"

"Control another body. You can make a physical body move around in the real world."

"Like you did on the sub? Where you were sitting there for awhile, and then you ate something?"

"Yes, like that."

"I guess it would be rude to ask where you go?"

"Yes, but we don't mind you being rude when you're learning. And I go different places."

"Like back home."

"No. I never go there." Amy's face closed, like she was not interested in talking about that.

Amon looked like he wasn't sure he should pursue this discussion. He went over to the Beetle and opened the door. He stood for a moment, and Amy could see he was smelling the interior.

"They don't make them like that anymore," remarked Amy, both meaning it and being slightly ironic.

"They don't?" Amon seemed genuinely surprised.

"No. That smell? They stopped making cars that smell like that. Just that smell alone will take many people back in time."

Amon looked at her sharply.

"Not literally back in time. It will bring back such strong memories that they'll feel like they've been transported to an earlier time."

"What about the sight of it?"

"Well, they DO make cars that look kind of like that now. And sight isn't as strong a memory trigger as the olfactory." She picked a stalk of wheat and popped some kernels in her mouth.

"Why is that?"

"The two parts of your brain that are involved in memory and involved in smell are close to one another."

"So just because they're juxtaposed, they influence each other?"

"Not JUST because. But yes, their proximity does play a part. The olfactory sense is part of the limbic system. That system interacts with memories and emotions. But it doesn't interact as strongly with the cognitive or language parts of the brain. So smells make you remember things and feel things, but they don't make you think about or talk about things as much as other forms of sensory perception." She handed Amon a stalk and he twirled it.

"So how does that relate to animals?"

"That's an interesting point."

"I like how you take my dumb questions and turn them into interesting points."

"Sometimes you get out of it what you put into it."

"Just sometimes?" He bit off the head and chewed experimentally. He shook his head and spit it out.

"Yes. There are many times you get far more out of something than you put in."

"Got it. So what fascinating point did I make about animals?"

"You brought up the fact that for many animals, smell is far more important than sight."

"Like dogs?"

"That's one of many examples. And they do relate smell to memory. That's why they trust the smell of some people and not others."

"I always thought they smelled fear."

"Well, they don't smell fear itself. But they smell what your body does when it's afraid."

"So how is that the same as trusting you because of memory?"

"It's not. There are many reasons why an animal chooses to trust a person… or decides not to."

"Memory being one… smelling your fear hormones being another?"

"Yes. And something you'll find that all animals including humans do really well is recognizing patterns." Amy looked intently at the head of another stalk of wheat as she said this.

"You're calling humans animals?"

"Yeah, an animal is defined as an organism that eats organic matter, has senses, and responds to stimuli. That definition fits humans."

"I thought humans were separate from animals."

"We are different from other animals. But according to the definition, we're still animals."

"So that means we evolved? Does that mean not believing that God made us?"

"That doesn't mean that. Some people think we evolved. Some think God made us through evolution. And others think that God made us without evolution."

"Which one is right?"

"Good question."

"How can that still be a question?"

"Meaning?"

"You can time travel. You can go back and SEE what happened!"

"Well, we did. But that CAUSED as many questions as it answered."

"How did it do that?" Amon sat down in the seat of the Beetle. Amy sat on the hood. A cool German breeze tossed her hair. The sun made the whole scene feel both palpably real and slightly ephemeral at the same time.

"Because we're not sure what the past looked like before time travelers went back. There are now civilizations that go back thousands of years."

"So the idea of God creating the world in six days must be wrong..."

"Why is that?"

"Because that would mean the world would only be about 6,000 years old, right?"

"Depending on how you interpret the first few verses of the Bible, if you mean the Christian view."

"But you just said that there are civilizations that go back longer than that?"

"There are. But were they there before time travel took us back? Did you watch that show "100"?"

"No."

"Oh, well, it wasn't fantastic, just OK. But the premise is that the Earth is getting overpopulated in the future, so they send people back in time to the time of dinosaurs, when there was plenty of room for everyone to live."

"And that happened in real life?"

"Not exactly. People weren't sent back because we needed room.

But people DID go back and start civilizations."

"That's where the Egyptians came from?"

"They were influenced, yes. But they came up with most of their culture without any help."

"That seems to argue against evolution."

"It does seem to. But it depends on who you ask. Some Ui believe in God. Some don't. Some are pretty agnostic."

"What if you go to times in history when there were supposed to be miracles? Doesn't that answer the question?"

"There are almost always logical, scientific explanations for things."

"So that means that there really isn't a God?"

"Every circumstance is open to interpretation. Two people can watch the same event take place, and one will tell you that it is undeniable proof God exists, and the other will tell you there is a scientific explanation for everything and no need to have superstitious beliefs."

"Which camp do you fall into?"

"We'll talk about that later. It's not good to bring up matters of belief too soon."

"OK."

Amy got her far off look suddenly.

"What's up?" asked Amon.

"Oh. I just got a message from Dorian. He wants us to come to the discussion room."

"For what?"

"He didn't say."

They returned from virtual Germany and went down the hall to the discussion room. There were several people seated around the big room. The walls were flowing ivory. A hint of vanilla was in the air. Amon could see the walls reflected in the smooth as glass polished marble floor, even though it was currently ink black.

"Do the rooms always change? I thought it looked different when we were in here earlier."

Amy nodded. "Yes, they change each day. It helps you keep track of when days change, since it can be easy to lose track."

Amy went to a chess board and sat down. Amon sat across from her and studied the board. There was a game in progress. He wondered who she was playing. Amon looked around the room and realized he knew many of the people present.

Eric was sitting backwards in a chair near the chessboard. Dorian and Serena were sitting on a couch that ran along the wall to Amon's left. The Atachis were here. Amon had only glimpsed them in the sub. Now he saw that they were all 4'11" tall, with black hair and gorgeous Japanese features. Three men and two women, all of them looking like they were around 22 years old, give or take. Amon guessed they were probably thousands of years old in reality.

He saw a powerful, angry looking African American man sitting next to Serena. He caught Amy's eye and asked who he was.

"Strode, this is Amon. Amon, Strode."

Strode leaped to his feet and charged across the room. He gripped Amon's hand, who barely had time to stand up before he was locked in the fierce gaze and powerful grip. "I'm glad you're here, man," said Strode. "You're going to do some pretty amazing things."

"That's what they tell me," laughed Amon. Strode looked at him intently, shook his hand, and went back to his seat. Amon was surprised he shook his hand instead of just holding it like everyone else seemed to do.

Eric laughed. "And what are we involved in today, my liege?"

Dorian said, "I used to hate when Eric called me that, but it has morphed over the centuries into a term of such hard won affection that I don't even hardly hear it anymore," he explained to Amon. Then he turned to the group and sighed. "It looks like Alisha needs help," Dorian said.

"What a surprise!" exclaimed Serena. "I can't remember when she didn't need our help. And that's saying something." That really was. Serena was the member of the group with the best ability at memory. As her name conveyed, Serena had a rare talent for calm and unflappability. This tranquil demeanor allowed her to spend much greater time in the SensDep pods, where the Ui meditated, focusing on tiny details with near-infinite patience. The result was close to perfect recollection of every event in her life.

Serena was extremely good at Monitoring, due to this patience and calm. But she wasn't the best. To her immense consternation, Alisha was actually the best at this.

Eric grinned "I'll bet Isha could tell you when the last time was." Serena smiled with her lips, but it didn't reach her eyes. Her tranquil surface sometimes had some powerful undercurrents.

Serena asked, "Are we going to explain that she can't keep doing this, or are we just going to let her keep causing--"

"You know the plan," said Dorian, quietly and forcefully. Now everyone looked at the ground. The echoes of 10,000 conversations reverberated in the room.

Amon was the only one not boring holes in the marble floor with his eyes. He looked back and forth between his new friends and asked the only question he could think of. "Does she do this often?"

Everyone smiled except Amy. Serena's eyes even twinkled a little. "Yes," Dorian explained, "she does this all of the time."

"How did she get into trouble?" asked Amon innocently. He stood up without realizing it and walked toward Dorian as he asked.

Everyone looked at Dorian for the answer that everyone already knew. "She has a hard time staying away from Them," Dorian intoned quietly.

"The DaiUi?" Amon asked. "Is she... does she want to... join them?"

"No," said Dorian. "She is one of us, and always has been. She just has a weakness for..."

"The bad boys," said Amy, sitting quietly at the chessboard, her eyes lost in the pawns.

"So help me understand this..." Amon looked from face to face, "We are going to help Alisha even though most of you seem to think this is a bad idea?"

Three of the Atachi gang sighed. The other two ran their hands through their jet black hair. Strode stood up. "Look, Amon," he said, his dark bass voice echoing through the room. "You have to understand how things work with the group."

"Ja, I get that," said Amon, his German accent becoming more prominent in his excitement, "that's what I'm trying to understand. How does it work?" Amon sat down on one of the giant plush bean bags and folded his arms.

"Dorian is in charge. He listens to all of our thoughts and concerns and questions and stuff," Strode sometimes seemed angry even when he wasn't, "and he really does take it into consideration, even when it seems like-"

"So he's the top guy??" asked Amon.

"...even when it seems like he doesn't," finished Strode, who hated to be interrupted. "But he has final say, at least right now. He's not the top guy. He's the third. The first and second are out on mission. And the main man, the top guy, has been captured by the DaiUi." Strode sat back down across from Amy at the chessboard and glanced at the formation of pawns. He frowned. Amon realized he was the one playing her.

"So Dorian is the top guy right now. Until one of the other two get back, or we rescue our top guy," said Serena.

"Do these guys have names?" asked Amon.

"Yes, but we're not going into that right now. For one thing, we give out information as people are ready for it," which sounded a whole lot like "when you need to know" to Amon, "and for another thing, you won't be meeting any of them for a long time," said Serena, smiling cryptically.

"By 'a long time', do you mean ..." Amon trailed off.

"Yes. Probably longer than many countries will exist," Serena nodded.

Amy caught his eye and mouthed, "David." She winked.

"So you all said that you don't think we should help Alisha, but Dorian overruled?" he asked, a little incredulous.

"Yes and no," said Serena, glancing at Amy. "Eric thinks we should go help her, but mostly just because he's itching for a fight." Eric grinned and spread his hands helplessly. "And Dorian is only doing what he knows our beloved leader would want. When we discussed this as a group, Dorian was against letting Isha come back over and over again. He thought we should draw a line and let her hit rock bottom."

"Which she has, again and again," said Dorian.

"Yes, and every time she does, she drags us down with her," said Serena quietly.

Eric stood up. "Well we're not going to sit around rehashing ancient discussions, are we? I think Dorian has made it clear that we're going to go rescue Isha. Let's get going." He popped a few gummy bears in his mouth from the bowl on the table.

Everyone looked at Dorian. "Where is she?" asked Serena.

"She's at Land's End," said Dorian quietly.

"You've GOT to be kidding me," said Serena. "WHEN is she?"

"She sent us a rescue beacon from 2008. She needs us to come and rescue her at that time. She's at Land's End and we need to come to June 12, 2008 to get her."

"Well, that'll be EASY", said Serena sarcastically.

"What's Land's End?" asked Amon.

"It's one of the biggest and best guarded strongholds of the DaiUi. There are dozens of guards and it is more or less impregnable," volunteered Kuri, one of the female Atachis. She didn't have a Japanese accent, but sounded like most everyone in the Ui, speaking English with just the slightest British accent.

"So how do we get in?" asked Amon. Dorian smiled, and even Amy glanced over at him. Her eyes moved around his face, seeking the motivation behind this offer.

"You're volunteering to go on the rescue mission?" asked Eric probingly.

"Well, she needs us, ja?" asked Amon.

"It's great that you are willing to go. But you've got about 1,000 years of training ahead of you before you're ready for a mission," intoned Dorian. "You'll stay here with me, and you'll be training." Everyone seemed like this was a forgone conclusion.

"So I'm just going to sit here and train while someone needs our help? In a matter of life and death??" Amon asked incredulously, getting back up again and standing by Eric.

"That's the thing about time travel, my friend," said Eric, clapping Amon on the shoulder and causing him to stumble forward. "It takes the immediacy out of 'saving the world'. It doesn't matter if we leave right this second or 5,000 years from now. We'll still be going back to the same time, to do the same mission."

"But won't the DaiUi have time to wreak more havoc if we delay?" asked Amon uncertainly, trying to wrap his brain around the idea of procrastinating in time travel.

"The DaiUi won't have any more or any less time regardless of when we leave," said Kuri. She seemed to be taking an interest in Amon, which of course meant that all of the Atachis were warming to him. The group of Japanese brothers and sisters seemed to share consciousness somehow. Amon was very interested in learning more about them.

"OK... I guess I'll get it one day," Amon said, shaking his head.

"Some of it doesn't make any sense no matter how long you think about it," said Strode. "You just kind of learn the rules and operate by them."

The Atachis, Serena, Strode, Eric, and a couple dozen people Amon had not yet met went to one wall of the room. Kuri opened a concealed panel and the wall slid aside to reveal mission gear. Everyone started suiting up and filling up their packs with items they would need. Amon saw a few devices that looked like small guns.

"Do you take weapons with you?" he asked.

"Yes, but not the kind you're thinking of," said Dorian, who was standing next to him watching the team suit up. "Anyone care to demonstrate?"

As if the whole thing had been staged and choreographed, Kuri turned with an impish grin and shot Eric with one of the tiny "guns". He went rigid, and then vanished. Kuri turned and handed Amon a sphere about the size of a tennis ball. It was shiny and white, and seemed to weigh nothing.

"Ah, a Sphere…finally I get to find out what they are!! What is this?" Amon asked, turning it around in his hands.

"That's Eric," she said, grinning. "He hates it when I do that."

"What did you do to him?"

"This is the first step that the DaiUi take to banish one of us," explained Dorian. "First they Sphere us. Then they send the Sphere out into the void, what people call 'outer space', and usually they do it through the Time Stream, so they don't know where they are or even WHEN they are. And they're trapped inside of the Sphere, which moves every time they move. So they can't touch the sides. This basically means they're trapped until someone rescues them. They can move, but since the Sphere moves with them, they can't see where they are, and the Sphere is designed to pull to one side, so if you keep moving, you go in circles. When the Ui Sphere an enemy, usually the DaiUi, we keep them here and keep them company, otherwise they self-terminate."

"But when the DaiUi sphere one of US, they usually shoot us out into the void. That's what happened to our 'top guy'. He's out in the void somewhere, somewhen, and we haven't found him yet…" said Serena, having finished suiting up and filling her pack.

"Which is what is eating at Isha," murmured Dorian.

"Alisha had plenty eating at her before that..." said Serena.

Dorian's face looked pained and he said nothing. Amon sensed the weight he was carrying. He felt for him.

"How could Eric possibly be in this tiny little ball that weighs nothing?" Amon asked, tossing the ball back and forth between his hands.

"He's very small now," grinned Kuri. She grabbed the ball from his hands and tossed it into the air. Aka spun and shot the little ball with a tiny gun of his own. The little Sphere exploded and Eric popped back into existence, rolling nimbly to his feet though he first appeared mostly upside down.

"Not my first rodeo," he said, winking at Amon. Amon wasn't sure what to think about that.

The group finished suiting up and headed for the door. Amon followed them. He wanted to see how exactly they were going to leave for this rescue mission. Dorian walked along beside Amon out the door and down the hall.

"I thought you weren't going on this mission?" asked Amon.

"I'm not. I'm headed to a meeting. A much needed one." said Dorian, looking very much in need of something. He seemed to be carrying leadership on his shoulders like Atlas.

"Who are you meeting?"

"The Others."

"Do you have to time travel to meet them?"

"No, they're in this time, and out of it," Dorian said paradoxically. "They exist outside of our space and time. But they can communicate with us no matter where or when we are."

"What about how or who or why you are?" asked Amon, familiarity making him feel a little silly.

Dorian's mouth turned up a tiny fraction at one corner. "Yes, no matter what we are, either, thankfully."

Amon wondered how much Dorian was humoring him and how much he was saying something profound. He guessed it was a pretty mixed bag.

Eric had the bowl of gummy bears in his hand, and was popping them in his mouth one after another as they went down the hall. Serena gave him a look.

"What?" he asked around the bears in his mouth.

"I … have an idea." She looked at the bears in the bowl, opened a pouch in her gear, and poured some in.

They exited the hallway into the fountain room. All of the team members dove into the fountain. The splashes which Amon expected from each person entering the water were a little subdued. Even Eric's huge frame disappeared beneath the surface of the water with hardly a sound.

Dorian turned to Amon. "Once I enter the pool, feel free to stay and look at the fountain if you'd like. But your training will begin shortly after. Just head back to the discussion room where we just were and your trainer will meet you there. She might not be there immediately, so wait until she comes."

"OK, *danke*," said Amon.

"You're welcome. I'm really glad you're finally here, and I'm pleased to see you are so inquisitive. You'll learn how things work here much more quickly than many do, who seem to resist the things they find instead of being open to them. You seem to embrace change pretty readily, and that will make your transition much smoother. Just don't give up on the training. I can tell you're used to getting things quickly, understanding without much effort. You're naturally good at things, and that will be your biggest challenge. Learn to wait. Learn to be bad at things, and be OK with that. The rest will follow."

Dorian walked swiftly to the fountain, dove over the little wall, and vanished from sight. As he had suggested, Amon walked to the fountain and looked into the depths of the swirling water. It was very difficult to make anything out, as the waters were constantly moving and foaming and changing. But he thought he glimpsed tiny figures moving around deep below the surface. Too far below, unless the fountain were miles deep. This didn't seem possible, but much of what Amon had seen since arriving had seemed impossible.

Amon stood staring into the swirling water for what seemed only a few moments. But he gradually became aware that someone was in the room with him. He turned slowly and saw an incredibly beautiful young woman. She was standing slightly behind him, and was also staring into the fountain. She wore a white robe very much like the one he was wearing.

For a long time, no one said anything. The woman stared into the water, and Amon watched her stare. After many breaths, she turned and looked Amon in the eye. He wasn't sure he'd ever seen anyone or anything as beautiful as she was. Her jet black hair was pulled back into a clasp at the back of her neck. Her skin looked tan, but it seemed as though she were tan all of the time. He suspected she might have middle-eastern or Indian ancestry.

"I'm Amon," he said, feeling foolish.

"I know," she said. "I'm here to keep you company until your trainer arrives."

"Oh. How long will that be?"

"I don't know, but if I know Dorian and his understatements, it could be awhile. I don't think anyone should have to wait alone for something they haven't ever experienced. It seems cruel to me.

Maybe that's just me."

"Is it going to be hard, the training?"

"Yes. But you'll grow into it. You'll begin to enjoy it, once you've hit your groove."

"How long will the training go on?"

"That's a difficult question to answer," she said. "Time is different here than where you're from. In a sense you'll never finish your training. When you are good at something, you'll want to keep training at it to get better, to become the best. When you're bad at something, you'll feel like quitting, but those are the lessons you need the most. Not just to gain proficiency... some of the things you'll be bad at are things you won't NEED to know how to do. But it's good for you to be bad at something and keep learning it anyway. It keeps your ego in check and grows your humility."

Amon looked back at the fountain. "Will they be gone long?"

"It's natural for you to ask questions like that, but you'll start to learn that they don't make a lot of sense here. It might seem like a few seconds or it might seem like eons... you'll learn to stay occupied while you wait for things like that. It's very good for you to keep your mind occupied. It's one of the chief weapons we have against the DaiUi."

"Weapons? I thought we tried to 'build bridges' with them," Amon asked dubiously.

"Yes, we do. But we use weapons to protect ourselves, not to attack. Maybe a better word would have been defenses. In any case, if you get antsy and bored, you put yourself in a position of weakness and the DaiUi will jump on that," she said.

Amon looked at her carefully. "I didn't catch your name. What did you say it was?"

"I didn't. But my name is Alisha."

Chapter Five

Amon looked nonplussed. "You're Alisha?? But... they just left to rescue you! What are you doing here??" Amon rushed to the fountain and looked in, apparently trying to communicate to the team that they should come back. He of course had no way of doing anything of the sort.

"You'll get used to this eventually," Alisha said quietly. "They ARE rescuing me. But I came here before I was captured to talk to you. I heard you were being trained today and I thought you could use some company. I was once here, waiting to be trained, and it didn't go so well. I got bored, and distracted... and I developed some bad habits."

"The... bad boys?" asked Amon helpfully.

Alisha sighed. "They've always been my weakness, since I was a little girl. I used to be what the other girls called 'boy crazy'. It probably had something to do with... well, my family was pretty messed up. I was ... hurt when I was a little girl. And then when I entered my teens, I had boyfriend after boyfriend, and even when I was serious about one of them, I found myself cheating on him with other boys. It's not something I'm proud of... I really wish I could ... I don't know. I don't even know why I'm telling you this. I just wanted you to..." She gave Amon a soul-piercing look. "I didn't want you to be alone today. So when I heard you were being trained, I came to sit with you and wait until your trainer came. Once she comes, I'll go back to when I came from, and they'll grab me, and I'll be at Land's End needing to be rescued."

"Why don't you just stay here and not go back? Then you won't get grabbed and won't need rescuing?" asked Amon sensibly.

"If only it were that easy..." she said, staring into the swirling water again.

Amon figured this was a girl thing and he wouldn't be understanding it sooner than he understood time travel, so he let it go. "What is the hardest part about … being part of the Ui?"

"For me? Or for most people?" asked Alisha.

Amon thought about it. "For me," he asked.

Alisha bit her lip. She looked at Amon, square in the face. This made Amon very nervous, as he hadn't had someone so beautiful stare him in the eye before. He felt every flaw in his face magnified 1,000 times.

"I think you will always be beating yourself up for what you can't do," said Alisha, frowning slightly.

"I thought we could do anything?" asked Amon.

"There's anything, and there's anything. You can perform any action you can think of. You can be smaller than a flea. You can fly. You can dive into a volcano. You can't be killed, and unless you lower your defenses, you can't even be hurt," Alisha explained.

"So why would I ever beat myself up?"

"Because you can't do things that are intrinsically contradictory," said Alisha.

"Like be two places at once?" he asked.

"No, you can do that. But you can't make a brick that's too big for you to pick up. See how it contradicts? You can do one or the other. Either you can pick up every brick, or you can make a brick no one can lift. You can't do both," she explained.

"Why would I..." he started.

"It's an example. But it means that you can't always win, even though you can DO ANYTHING... see how that works? When you're fighting against MORTAL people, you will almost always win. People are wily, though, and they'll surprise you. But you're smarter, stronger, faster... everything you need to almost always win. But when you're dealing with the DaiUi... they're just as smart, fast and strong as you are."

"Like Superman fighting the other people from his planet," said Amon.

"You know Superman?"

"We Germans know the *ubermensch*."

"That's part of it. Another part is your inner struggles. You will still have temptations... you will still have moral weaknesses. And your immortality and invincibility make these temptations that much more difficult."

"Because no one can stop you."

"Now you're starting to get it. When I start feeling that pull... and I get a certain guy in my head... there's nothing anyone can do to stop me. There's not a jail that'll hold me...I can't be stopped. I can't even stop myself. That's the problem," she said, choking on the last words.

"I'm sorry. I think I get it."

"Yeah, I think you do. But just wait until the thing inside of me that betrays me betrays YOU," she said, looking into the waters again. "You might not be so understanding."

Amon started to put his arm around her, but her beauty frightened him too much. He started the movement and then aborted halfway through, making a strange and awkward movement. Alisha sensed what he intended and moved over to him, wrapping her arms around his middle. He clumsily put his arms around her. His heart was racing embarrassingly. Her head was against his chest and she seemed so fragile and small. He wanted to protect her from... from the thing inside her that had been trying to destroy her all of her life.

"Just stay here," said Amon.

Alisha laughed and sobbed in one explosive gasp. "That's what I've been telling myself for thousands of years..."

They stood like that for what seemed even longer.

Then they heard a female throat being cleared meaningfully. Amon immediately let go and tried to pull away. Alisha held on a few seconds longer, rubbed Amon's back gratefully, and let go. She walked over to the fountain without looking back and dove in with perfect grace.

Chapter Six

Amon turned around feeling guilty and saw a young lady that looked to be about 20 to 25 years old, but there was no telling how old she was. Amon was sure she was at least as old as she looked... but was probably much, much older.

"Hello, Amon. Are you ready to get started?" she asked. She didn't smile, but her manner seemed very amiable.

"I guess so. You have me at a loss. You know my name..."

"You can call me Maria. That's what people today call me. My original name is very difficult for people of this time to pronounce."

"May I hear it?" asked Amon politely.

She pronounced her name, given to her thousands of years previously. It had some sounds in it that were faintly Arabic sounding. And she was right... Amon could not reproduce that sound in 100 tries.

"Maria it is," he said. He smiled apologetically.

"If you want to come with me, we'll begin your training," she said, walking toward the door.

"Right this second?" he asked, a little startled.

"No time like the present," she said, and almost winked.

They walked down the hallway, passed the room where the group had previously met to discuss the mission, and entered what vaguely resembled a gym. There was a swimming pool with several rather ominous looking tanks in it. A great deal of climbing equipment was scattered around the enormous room. And one wall was lined with big black pods.

They walked to one of the pods. Maria placed her hand on the surface of the pod just off center, and an unseen door slid open in the side of the pod. The pod was about eight feet tall. It was shaped vaguely like a pear. It was so intensely black that looking at it for any length of time made Amon feel a little disoriented and dizzy. His brain didn't know what to make of something that reflected no light at all.

"We'll begin with some simple meditation. Nothing too stressful to start off with. We need to develop some trust between us as trainer and student, and guided meditation is a good way to ease into that trust relationship. I'm going to get into the pod next to this one, as you enter yours here. I suggest you step in and hang your robe on this hook by the pod door. Then you can retrieve it when you're done with the exercise. I'll be guiding you by voice alone from the pod next to yours. Is all of that clear? Any questions?"

Amon thought for a second, shook his head, and stepped into the pod. Maria disappeared as she walked to her pod. He slipped out of the robe and dropped it like she said. Then, fully naked, he looked around the inside of the pod. There was water in the bottom of the pod, and it was just warm enough that he could barely feel that it was there. He was just beginning to wonder what to do next when Maria's voice came to him from all around, very gentle but perfectly audible.

"Alright, to start, lie down in the water and wait for the door to close."

Amon did so, feeling awkward and exposed. He floated in the salty warm water for a few minutes and heard only the sound of his own breathing.

Maria's voice came over the speakers finally... "Just relax. Try not to think too hard. Just float and listen to your breathing. I'll speak to you from time to time... but mostly just listen to your breathing and let your body relax completely. It helps if you imagine the parts of your body, starting with your toes and working your way up your body, and thinking about them relaxing and loosening and soaking into the water... "

Amon did as she suggested, and gradually his body seemed almost to fade out of existence.

Chapter Seven

The team swam through the viscous air streams, following the Atachi team. They were the best at finding the right time to leave the Stream. Leaving the Stream is something that took great timing and practice, and most people miss the time they're aiming for by several years. Some miss by decades, and people have even missed by centuries. Getting back into the stream once you leave is possible, but extremely tricky. So leaving at the right time was very important.

The Atachis possessed a very rare ability to leave the stream within just a few days of the target time.
It had something to do with their perfect groupthink. Seeing the Stream outlets from multiple perspectives simultaneously probably gave them better accuracy in choosing the precise moment to jet. Whatever it was, they were good.

So everyone else took their lead and followed them out of the stream when they left. Following them wasn't hard, since all of the Ui (except a few, including the newly received Amon) could speed themselves up (or slow down time, depending on how you thought about it) and respond to actions to the 1000th of a second. So when the Atachis dodged out of the stream, the rest of the team followed instantly.

They arrived at the Australian portal 56 months and 3 days before the date they were told by Dorian.
Now, they just had to travel from their arrival location, near Perth, to the DaiUi stronghold known as Land's End, which was located on a tiny island off the coast of New Zealand. They needed to get there very quietly, without being noticed. The best way to accomplish this was to travel small.

So the entire team agreed to shrink themselves to being smaller than a grain of sand. Each of them opened their viewer and clicked on the icon that shrank them. Then they hit the water. They traveled under water across the Great Australian Bight, passed Tasmania, and headed out across the Tasman Sea to the south of New Zealand. A few minutes later, they were approaching Adams Island, just to the south of Auckland Island. They entered the channel at the south of the island and traveled across the bottom of the channel, moving erratically to make detection more difficult.

The team emerged near the head of the channel and regrouped. They entered the Land's End compound while the DaiUi watched every step they took.

Bronty, the leader of the outside team, was coming to grips with the pain of losing Amon and Amy. He was covered in tattoos on every inch of his skin, visible and invisible. He was sad about losing his two dumb companions, who were Sphered due to the team's failure in the Nazi sub.

He had the artwork done before becoming one of the Ui decades ago. He opted to keep it, even though changing his appearance was an easy possibility. At the time, the Ui took this as a mark of humility and a desire to see his former life fulfilled in his immortal one. But when Bronty joined the DaiUi, the artwork took on a more sinister meaning.

Bronty told his team, all two dozen of them, that they should get ready to strongly and painfully repel the attempted impregnation of their location. They picked up the team on their sensors when they entered the channel. They hid themselves in pockets around the compound's entrance, waiting for the Ui team to show themselves.

It wasn't long before they did. Moving swiftly and quietly, the Ui team dispersed in a classic approach formation, ducking behind trees and shrubs and small buildings as they came closer to the side entrance, which was only visible to the Ui team because they knew where it was. Bronty knew that the Ui knew where it was, since not that long ago he was planning just such strategies with them. He knew exactly where they would come from, how they would space their advance and how they would cover each other as they came. It would not have been easier to predict their movements if he had actually sat in on their planning session earlier that day.

There were a few movements that the team made that were clearly intended to throw him off of their intent. But he expected that. Of course they wouldn't just use the exact same plan that they knew he knew. And coming across the bottom of the channel was not something they had discussed when he was Ui. It was also clearly designed to try to get them past his surveillance.

Using silent mental commands, Bronty instructed his team to hold back until the Ui got much closer. He didn't want to spook them and cause them to abort their attempt. Bronty's superiors had worked far too hard to trap Alisha so that the Ui would come trying to make a rescue attempt. If Bronty screwed it up by scaring them off before he could Sphere them, he would have some explaining to do.

The Ui team converged on the side entrance, dropping a couple guards with sleeper holds. This was exactly what Bronty was expecting, even hoping, they would do. Once they entered the vestibule, he would spring his trap.

He saw that Strode was left outside as warning sentinel, which surprised him a little. Strode was very effective in a close fight, almost as adept a fighter as Eric, and Bronty didn't expect him to be left outside to sound alarm when anyone could do it as easily. Maybe this was done to throw him off the trail as well. It made him a little nervous though, since he didn't know exactly what to make of it. He decided to take Strode out himself, to minimize the risk of losing the prize that Strode would make when he'd been Sphered.

Bronty moved stealthily to that side of the entrance and slipped up silently behind Strode. He waited for one of his team to make a loud distraction noise, and during the noise he shot Strode with his Spheregun. Strode froze, then popped into a tennis ball sized Ping-Pong ball looking object. Bronty scooped it up, having trouble believing how easy it had been. That's when he saw that one of the Atachis, Kuro it appeared to be, was guarding Strode's back. The little ninja like member of the Ui team dropped from the tree where he'd been hiding and in less than half of a second had Bronty on the ground in a hold. He was pulling his Sphere gun to trap Bronty when one of Bronty's team members caught Kuro in a lucky shot and another white Ping-Pong ball slipped into Bronty's pocket. That was a close one, and he wasn't going to take any more chances.

He gave the order for both of his teams to enter the vestibule and to enter firing. He heard the report of their Sphereguns and he heard shouts. One of the Atachis appeared from nowhere behind Bronty, swiped his legs out from under him, and took the two Ping-Pong balls from his pocket. He then disappeared as suddenly as he had appeared. He heard some good news from the vestibule, though. Both teams reported that they only lost one man to being Sphered, but they had managed to catch the entire Ui team in their crossfire, and the whole team was now comprised of a couple dozen Spheres which were now bagged up and headed back to Bronty. The only one missing from this total victory was whichever Atachi had swiped the two Spheres from his pocket.

He sprinted to the vestibule and met the team when he was almost there. They handed him the bag with the Spheres in it. He took it in stride and entered the vestibule. He palmed the security scanner and spoke his code phrase. The inner door opened and Bronty navigated the hallways quickly with two of his team members flanking him. The rest of his teams returned to surveil the surrounding area.

Bronty went to the leader of Land's End. He placed the bag containing the Spheres on the floor near a small pool. He reached into the bag and pulled out Sphere after Sphere, dropping them into the pool. They floated on the surface, looking like bubbles.

Bronty looked up at his leader. He waited for him to speak. The man had his eyes closed and seemed to be in some kind of meditative state. But Bronty knew that the man was aware of everything happening in the room, in the building, and throughout Land's End. Bronty also knew that his leader enjoyed making him wait. Bronty was not a patient person, but he knew the consequences of interrupting, so he waited, fidgeting while he did so.

What seemed like days later, the man sitting on a bamboo mat on the raised dais opened his eyes. He stared at Bronty for a very long time. Bronty hated that, too. The man on the mat was very small. He looked Asian, but Bronty wasn't sure what nationality. He only went by one name – Oko.

Oko finally spoke. "You let three of them escape."

Bronty nodded. He knew that no matter how successful his missions were, he would always pay for what he didn't do. It was how it worked. How Oko worked.

"We will deal with your punishment later. For now, I want you to double check our primary prisoner and ensure that the perimeter is secure. Then I want you to unSphere our guests."

Bronty was relieved. He knew his punishment would be severe, but he was glad to be out of the room and back on duty, at least for the moment. He jogged down the hall to the room where Alisha was being kept in her Sphere. The Sphere was lying in its setting, looking like a giant pearl. Bronty checked in with each member of his team and discovered that the building was secure. He returned to Oko's room and knelt once more, waiting for the command to unSphere the prisoners. He wasn't sure that was the best idea, but Oko knows what Oko knows.

Oko didn't make Bronty wait long this time. Bronty suspected it was because Oko was as eager to see their new captives as he was. But Bronty still didn't have any idea how they were supposed to contain them once they were unSphered. How could Bronty keep them from shrinking and vanishing?

Oko nodded to Bronty and Bronty turned to the little white orbs floating on the surface of the pool. He shot the first one with his Spheregun and it popped. Something small and red floated on the surface of the pool for a second, and then began to sink. He looked at Oko, and noticed that Oko was watching Bronty's face, not the pool. This was not a good sign. He nodded again, clearly indicating with some impatience that Bronty should continue unSphering the rest of the little white balls.

He shot each of them, and each popped into a tiny object about the same size and shape, but different colors, and dropped into the pool, sinking eventually. Most Ui could zoom their vision in to see things on the microscopic level, even from a great distance. But Bronty's return to "creative substances" since he became DaiUi caused him to lose much of his visual control.

After he had shot the last Sphere, Oko motioned for him to go to the pool and investigate what Oko seemed already to know. Bronty moved to the pool, reached in, and plucked out one of the tiny objects, this one yellow. He lifted it out of the pool and saw that it was sticky and seemed to be melting. It had a sweet smell to it. It took him a moment to realize that he was holding a gummy bear.

He looked into the pool and saw that, sure enough, every Sphere had dispensed a gummy bear when it was shot. Some of them were almost completely dissolved now, but he could see the remnants of several where they were sinking slowly in the pool.

Bronty looked to Oko and saw that Oko knew already. WHEN Oko realized what had happened, that the Ui had tricked Bronty, was unclear. Bronty would probably never find out. He assumed it was not before the Ui arrived, or he was pretty sure Oko would have told him.

Oko gestured to the door, and one of the team came in carrying the setting in which Alisha's Sphere was ensconced. Bronty began to feel very cold and to sweat at the same time. He had a horrible sinking feeling in his gut, and he wondered how bad his punishment could be for this huge mistake.

Oko nodded again, indicating that Bronty should shoot Alisha's Sphere. He hesitated. Oko's expression grew slightly darker. Bronty had never seen that happen before, and it unnerved him. For the first time he could remember, he began to wonder if it was worth it being with the DaiUi. He began to think maybe he should give the Ui another try. Nothing could be worth this.

Bronty shot the Sphere, and expected to see a gummy bear in the setting. Instead, he was perplexed to find something oblong and brown. He moved closer, almost against his will, and picked up the object in his hand. He realized he was holding a chocolate Cadbury Egg.

Oko watched his face for a very long time. Bronty returned the egg to the setting. He knelt, waiting for Oko's decision.

He waited a long time.

Chapter Eight

The Ui team exploded out of the fountain, laughing uproariously. Amy's eyes danced and had a twinkle in them, as she climbed out of the fountain and looked at her companions. Eric was whooping and laughing like he was in the winning locker room at a high school football game. He kept picking everyone up (even Strode, who usually did not put up with such antics) and hugging them and kissing the tops of their heads. Serena's very reluctant, but very huge grin stretched from one ear to the other. The Atachis were more hyper than their usual calm selves, and no one seemed sure what they were doing exactly, but it seemed some kind of elaborate victory dance.

The rest of the team was laughing and passing around bottles of something of a dark brewed nature and were divesting themselves of their gear as they left the fountain room and headed back to the room where they suited up originally.

But no one was happier than Alisha. She was hugging everyone and laughing and thanking everybody over and over, crying and laughing at the same time.

"That was beautiful!" yelled Eric. "It went perfectly--"

"Except for the part where Strode and Kuro got Sphered!" exclaimed Serena.

"Yeah, that was a close one," smiled Kuro. "I thought we were in trouble."

"If that hadn't happened, though, I think Bronty might have been more suspicious. After all, we didn't change our approach that much from when he was Ui," said Amy.

"Yeah, he definitely fell for it, though. You should have seen his face when his peeps were shooting 'us' in the vestibule. He thought he'd won the lottery," beamed Strode.

Alisha had one arm around Kuro and one around Serena. Her smile sobered a bit, and she said "OK, so spill it. How did you manage to pull that off??"

The whole team left the fountain room and entered the discussion room. They all grabbed beverages and arranged themselves around the room, similar to before but this time with Alisha curled up on the couch.

Dorian, who apparently had returned from his visit with the Others, started the story, "Well, Buru has been working on his speed, as you know."

"He's always been the fastest Ui we've ever known," said Isha.

Dorian smiled, "Well, he's gotten faster. You know how with mortals, we can move so fast they can't even see us? Like we can enter a room and move things around and leave and they don't even know we were there? Because we're doing things in 1000th of a second?"

"Yeah?" said Isha.

"Well, Buru has gotten so fast, he can do that to US now. He can move so fast even WE can't see him," said Dorian, sounding like even he had trouble believing it.

"That's impossible," said Isha. "He'd have to be moving... I don't think anything can move that fast."

"Hold up your drink," said Dorian with a challenging smile.

Isha held her drink up.

"Watch your ice cubes closely," Dorian said.

She watched. One instant there were three cubes. Something happened, she sensed movement but couldn't put her finger on it, and suddenly there were only two cubes in her glass. The drink sloshed slightly, filling in the hole where the cube used to be.

She looked at Buru. He was smiling. He opened his mouth and popped an ice cube into his hand.

Chapter Nine

"Since I was stuck here 'holding down the fort'," said Val, "Why don't you walk me through how this went down? It sounds like you all had good time." His Russian accent was almost gone, but he still dropped his articles occasionally. Val was a huge blond bear of a man. He reclined on one entire couch himself. He seemed bored and sad for the most part, but perked up a little at the team's exuberance.

"Well, the plan was for Kuro alone to enter the area, and project holograms of the rest of the team for the DaiUi to shoot at. When they shot each one, Buru would place a Sphere in that place containing a gummy bear," explained Serena.

"But, and fortunately, the Strode hologram got shot himself. So Kuro 'rescued' him, then got Sphered HIMself. Buru had to come rescue him for real. Fortunately he was fast enough to replace all of the empty Spheres with gummy Spheres and rescue Kuro without being detected," she explained.

"While Kuro and Buru were keeping the teams busy, the rest of us snuck into the compound and replaced Alisha's Sphere with one containing a Cadbury Egg."

"Why Cadbury Egg?" asked Val. "Why that?"

"It's my favorite candy," said Isha.

"We just carried her Sphere out with us and didn't unSphere her until we were well away," Serena added.

"We think Oko was aware of the rescues, but wasn't able to stop us because he realized what was happening too late. Once he knew what was going on, we'd made all the replacements and were on our way back into the time Stream," Strode pointed out.

Val frowned. "But how did you get to Alisha and grab her Sphere?"

"We were traveling small and fast. They didn't expect us in the compound because they thought they were nabbing us in the vestibule. It was a classic case of *ofermod*," said Strode.

"*Ofermod* means 'overconfidence'," explained Serena, smiling indulgently. It seemed to amuse her seeing Strode use jargon. He had recently been studying medieval lit, and enjoyed sharing what he learned.

"So now that Isha is free, what's next on our agenda?" asked Eric, rubbing his hands together. He was clearly hoping for some action.

Dorian said, "I need two of you to join the sweep teams."

"We still haven't found him?" asked Alisha faintly.

"Not a trace. But don't worry, Isha. We'll find him," said Dorian.

"I want to join the sweep teams," said Alisha.

"I'm not sure-" started Dorian.

"You know how it works, Dorian," she replied quietly, "I'm no safer from myself here than I am out sweeping. And if I'm out there looking for him, maybe I'll stay sufficiently distracted."

To Serena's credit, she didn't even sniff.

Chapter Ten

Amon was floating in a sea of nothingness. He had been in this state for longer than his entire life, or so it seemed. He wasn't sure anymore. But, strangely enough, he wasn't remotely bored. It was as if every tiny little thing was immensely interesting all of the time. When all of his senses had been "removed" by the sensory deprivation chamber, his focus became razor sharp. Every syllable, every glottal stop and lip movement in every word that Maria spoke to him through the sound system was entirely captivating. The sibilants were engrossing. The fluidity of the vowels seemed to buoy him in the nothingness in which he floated. Even though the time he'd spent so far seemed like three of his former lifetimes, he never wanted it to end. He was, for the first time in his consciousness, entirely free from the distractions, not only of life, not only of his senses, but even of his own body. He seemed to be pure mind.

Maria's intonations carried him back to his childhood. He easily remembered several short vignettes. He pieced together more of the story with her coaching. He began to draw observations about large themes running through his life, seeing patterns he never noticed before. Maria nudged him back earlier and earlier, never pushing too hard, just edging him to remember things as early as thirty months old. Before that, no manner of urging could dredge up any memories.

After running back and forth through his life multiple times, he felt he had command of his own self for the first time in his life. He was at peace with his failures and weaknesses, neither ashamed of them nor feeling guilty for his mistakes and blunders. He saw who he really was, and accepted himself. It was an amazing feeling.

"OK, Amon, we're going to return to our bodies and our tanks now," her voice instructed gently. He really did feel as though he were coming back to his body after being away for a while, though he logically knew this wasn't the case. "Descend into your body and feel it wrap around you."

He descended. It wrapped. He felt the blood rush through his veins.

He sensed the air moving in and out of his lungs, through his throat, traversing his nostrils. He sensed his position in relation to "down" and "up". He sensed how his arms were akimbo and his legs were slightly bent. He didn't sense any temperature except a very slight coolness on his forehead. Even without seeing, hearing, tasting, smelling, or touching anything, he sensed plenty. He suddenly realized how silly the idea of five senses was.

He very gradually became aware of light in the chamber. It was very, very dim. About once per minute, it grew a little brighter. He heard very soft music begin to play, something classical. Unless he was mistaken, he thought it was Eine Kleine Nachtmusique. (He wasn't mistaken). The water in the chamber began to drain gradually, and he found himself drifting down onto a recliner chair, a chaise lounge. He was still for many breaths, maybe for minutes, maybe for hours. The music continued to play, growing a little louder each moment until it was at the level normally heard in an elevator. The light had gotten brighter and was now about what is found in a movie theater before the movie starts.

The door to the chamber opened, and Maria's face appeared in the opening. She smiled. She was wearing the white robe again. Amon was facing away from the door and realized he was still naked. Maria tossed his robe to him, and he caught it before it hit the draining water.

He put it on, cinched it with the belt, and stood up. He went to the door and stepped out.
"How long was I in there?" he asked.

"A few weeks," she said.

"Why aren't I hungry? Or thin? Or thirsty?"

"The fluid you were floating in wasn't just water. It had all of the nutrients and hydration that your body needs. You could float in that fluid for years and you would never get hungry, thirsty, or lack anything your body needs. And since you're now immortal, you would never age or die."

"How do you know this? Has anyone done it?" Amon asked.

"Yes. Serena has spent decades floating. She is amazingly adept at concentration and memorization."

"If she's so good at meditation, why does she always seem like she's seething when Alisha's name is mentioned?" asked Amon, genuinely curious.

"She's come a long way," said Maria, a very serious expression on her face, "you would not be able to imagine what she would be like if she didn't have such great control."

"Well, if it's anything like I imagine, she would most likely have killed Alisha by now."

Maria just smiled enigmatically.

"Your smile makes me think I'm not too far off the mark," said Amon with a question mark in his tone.

"Let's just say they're much better friends now than they've ever been before."

"So why does Dorian seem like he doesn't want to save her, either, but is doing it out of some weird sense of obligation?"

"Dorian is caught in the middle of a very complicated and ancient relationship."

"I'm not sure I've ever heard the words 'ancient' and 'relationship' used together like that before," remarked Amon.

"You'll get used to it. We've all spent centuries dealing with the questions you're asking. And we've come to terms with the way the things play out, even if we don't fully understand them, even after all this time."

"So does Dorian have feelings for Alisha?"

Maria sighed, and Amon could hear the millennia behind the sound. "We all have feelings for each other. Yes yes, I know what you mean. But in a sense, we all have deeper feelings than you can fathom for one another. Imagine the love, respect, comradery, jealousy, and pride that you feel for your brother, your mother, your wife, and your children all rolled into one gigantic feeling for one other person. Now imagine that you have ten times that feeling for every other member of the Ui. You have taken the first step toward understanding how we feel about each other. We all know each other so well... we care about each other so deeply... yes, even Serena cares that deeply about Alisha. But she still really wants to kill her sometimes."

"But does-"

"They were never together. But when you spend a thousand years with someone, you care about them in ways that transcend what you've ever experienced before. You go through the usual cycles of caring about them like a sibling... then you care about them more deeply, and usually you have romantic feelings. I've had romantic feelings for almost every member of Ui at one time or another. But then you go deeper than that. You move into the comfortable feeling that old couples have with one another. Of course, all along the way you go through stages of them driving you crazy. You know what they'll say before they say it. You know what they're thinking, even without the mental messaging going on."

"When do I start mental messaging?" asked Amon.

"You need to spend some serious time in the meditation chamber-"

"More serious than I just did??" he asked incredulously.

"You barely began to scratch the edge of the surface. You will spend several human lifetimes in that tank."

"I would normally balk at that idea, but I have to admit that I really enjoyed my time in there just now."

"And it gets better. It's tempting to want to just stay in there once you get going. Serena tells us she has to force herself to leave. It can be addicting."

"So why do I need so much chamber time before I can send mental messages?"

"Because you need to learn to control your thoughts. We don't share EVERYthing we're thinking. We choose to shoot messages to each other. If we let you mental message now, you would embarrass yourself every three seconds. But when you know someone as well as I was talking about, you move past the level of happy old couple into something that you've never even heard of, let alone experienced. You move into a level of deep intimacy. It's something that can't really happen in an ordinary human lifetime, because by the time you have known someone long enough for it to start happening, your body starts breaking down and you begin to die in earnest."

"That's a cheerful thought."

Maria laughed. "Yeah, it's a little morbid, I know. But with the Ui, you know someone very, very well for a very long time. And you inhabit a body that is unaffected by age or death. This produces a very deep connection between people that transcends anything you know of regarding relationships. You begin to see each other as part of yourself, yet still 'other'. You learn to depend on each other in a way that would be unhealthy in a normal mortal relationship."

"That sounds like it would make it especially painful when someone leaves."

"You have no idea."

Chapter Eleven

The crew sat around in the discussion room, talking about what the next plan would be. Alisha and Strode left to go do sweeps, looking for their leader. Amon and Maria heard the laughter and came in.

Eric had an enormous stein of ale which he quaffed with gusto. Amon sat down next to him and picked up a much smaller stein. "Mind if I have some?" he asked.

Eric looked at him dubiously. Then he shrugged and took the stein from Amon. He held it up to the end of a huge dark brown keg with a ceramic spigot gouged into the side of it. He turned the knob on the spigot and it made a squeak, after which thick black fluid gushed out, filling the smaller stein immediately.

Germany is known for its fantastic and varied brews, and Amon was no amateur when it came to the adult beverages. But he had never seen anything quite like this ale.

He inhaled the fumes rising from his stein. He blinked, and Eric watched him closely, smiling very slightly. Amon took a tiny sip and made a face like a baby taking a bite of a lemon. Eric watched even more closely, this being the moment of truth.

Amon swallowed. He exhaled through his nose and stared straight ahead for several minutes. Eric took a few swallows from his own stein, his eyes never leaving Amon's face.

Amon took a deep breath, steadied himself against the table, and took a larger drink from his stein. He put the stein down and slumped back in his chair. His eyelids drooped and his mouth opened in a tired pant.

"Good, huh?" asked Eric, finishing his enormous drink and refilling it.

Amon didn't reply. He stared ahead with drooping lids for several minutes, then he fell over onto the floor.

Chapter Twelve

The three teenage girls looked around nervously and giggled as they approached the hot tub. One of them kept her robe wrapped tightly around her and kept looking over her shoulder.

"Come on, Jen, it'll be fun," said Trish, shoving her good naturedly.

Jen tried to smile but it looked more like a grimace.

When they got to the tub, they noticed that there was a young man already soaking. Jen froze and started to turn back to their room. But the other two girls weren't having it. They each grabbed an arm and started pulling her toward the tub.

Jen apparently had enough of looking ridiculous, especially in front of an attractive young man, so she stopped fighting and sat down on one of the chairs by the hot tub.

The other two girls dropped their robes on the chairs and stepped down into the tub, glancing at the young man and smiling a little. He smiled back.

"Where did you say you got that bikini, Jess?" asked Trish.

"That store we went to last weekend... I can't remember the name of it. In the mall by Dillard's," said Jess.

"You coming in, Jen?" teased Trish, glancing at the young man again.

The young man smiled and said, "Water feels good, doesn't it?"

The girls looked at each other and giggled again. "Jess has to soothe her back every night," explained Trish confidentially.

Jen watched from her chair.

"Hey Jen, can you hand me the stuff in my robe pocket?" asked

Trish.

Jen looked unsure.

"Come on... touching it isn't gonna hurt you."

Jen reached into the robe, took out a blunt, and handed it to Trish along with a lighter.

Trish lit up and took a long drag. She handed it to Jess who did the same.

"Which of these things... doesn't belong here..." sang the young man to the old Sesame Street tune.

Jen looked unhappy, but the other two giggled again. "Yeah, she's a little uptight. We're trying to get her to loosen up," explained Jess.

"Why are you uptight, little girl?" asked the young man.

Jen looked around the pool area like she was hoping someone would come along and rescue her. She mumbled something unintelligible.

"It's ok. I see you're shy. Unlike your two friends here," the man said, smiling at Trish and Jess. They smiled back.

"No, we're not shy. We're way past shy," said Trish through a cloud of smoke. She looked over the young man's shoulder at the wall behind the hot tub. "There's a bug on the wall behind you," she said, giggling.

The man looked behind him and then turned back and smiled. "That's not a bug. That's my pal, Jiminy. Say hello Jiminy."

The cricket on the wall jumped onto the man's shoulder and made a chirping noise. From the way they laughed, apparently the girls thought this was the funniest thing they'd ever seen, and the young man wondered if the blunt was affecting their minds. Jen looked slightly horrified and moved her chair farther away from the tub.

"Does Jimmy talk to you?" asked Trish, moving closer to the young man.

"That little cricket gives me the best advice," said the young man seriously. The girls looked at each other and giggled nervously.

The man smiled self-deprecatingly and shook his head. "I'm just kidding."

The girls smiled again and moved a little closer.

"He actually gives me terrible advice," said the young man. In that instant, his face became very serious and hungry. His eyes widened and his mouth dropped open. The girls looked terrified, and Jen stood up.

The cricket jumped from the man's shoulder and landed on Trish's arm. She screamed like she was on fire, but in a silent stage whisper, and went rigid. The cricket jumped to Jess's forehead, and she too screamed silently, stiffening like she was having a seizure. Jen started to run, and the cricket launched itself from Jess's forehead and landed precisely between Jen's shoulder blades on her robe. She ran faster, seeming to feel its presence. It crawled up the back of her robe and she started to scream in earnest. But just as she drew her breath to scream, the cricket reached the back of her neck. Her body flew out, straight as a board, and she hit the grass face first.

The young man climbed slowly out of the tub, shaking his shoulder length blond hair and tugging his black trunks straight as he walked over to Jen. He grabbed her ankle and picked her whole body up with one hand, and carried her back to the tub with no more effort than if she had been an inflatable toy. The cricket jumped back onto his shoulder and chirped.

"No, Jiminy. I'm not going to hurt Jen. She intrigues me. I'm going to talk to Jen. As for the other two... I'll only be doing what they were going to do with me anyway. But I'll enjoy it a great deal more with them looking at me like they are right now." He looked at them with a curious gleam in his eyes, and they stared back at him, clearly terrified out of their minds but unable to move a muscle, not even to blink, not even to breathe. "You might want to loosen them up a little, Jiminy, before they suffocate."

He knew that Jiminy knew this already, but sometimes he thought that the little cricket was even more sadistic than he was.

Chapter Thirteen

Eric and Serena had just sat down to a game of chess when the alarm sounded.

"Security breach?" asked Serena incredulously. "Is that right?"

Eric checked the system on the wall. "YES!!!" he bellowed, with the biggest smile Serena had ever seen on his face.

"Hold on, Eric," she said. "We need to check with Dor-"

"I don't think we do, Ser!" he said, smiling even bigger. "We have standing orders. Anytime we have a security breach, we respond with force. Sphereguns if appropriate. It's time to bust some heads. FINALLY!!" he roared. He was clearly enjoying this.

Just then Dorian and three DaiUi entered the room from the hall. They saw Eric and halted in their tracks. "Dorian?" asked Eric. "What are you..." he stopped and looked at Dorian closely. Then he moved so fast it was impossible to follow, even for Serena. She knew he wasn't moving as fast as the Atachis could, but even with her perception up to speed, she couldn't follow his movements because they were totally unexpected. She was going to have to replay this over and over to follow exactly what happened.

The next thing Serena, Dorian, or the three DaiUi knew, everyone in the room was on the floor except for Serena. Dorian and the three DaiUi were pinned under Eric, who was telling Serena to get the Sphereguns immediately.

"What are you d-"

"Get them! Now!" he said.

But it was too late.

Chapter Fourteen

Strode and Alisha finished up sweeping known areas for holding Spheres in the year 1554 and moved to 1555. While it was possible to miss a time if you went year by year, it was unlikely. And the DaiUi usually kept Spheres in largely the same places – where they could keep an eye on them, and where they could torment the people who were Sphered. So while it still was rather like looking for a needle in a haystack, at least it wasn't like looking for a needle in all of the haystacks in the whole world.

The sweeps had proven successful so many times that the DaiUi had had to change their strategies and keep their Spheres in new places. But due to time travel, it was possible to look for Spheres before they had been moved. As long as the victim had not been Sphered in the last year or so, Strode and Alisha knew pretty much where to look. And the one they were looking for was taken a century ago.

So the two of them headed into 1555, sweeping the usual places and keeping their fingers crossed. Alisha even said a silent prayer... knowing she was the last one to deserve an answer.

Chapter Fifteen

The young man sat next to Jen in the hotel room. The cricket was chowing down in the kitchenette. Jen wasn't sure what it was eating, and didn't want to ask. Not that she could... she was still paralyzed. She could breathe and move her eyes, but that was about it.

The young man had carried her and the other two girls into the hotel room stacked up like... well, she wasn't sure what it was like. She'd never seen human beings transported like that before. He just put one on top of the other, picked up all three like they weighed nothing, and carried them across the pool area and down the hall to his room. They passed an Asian couple in the hallway and the couple acted like they didn't even see the young man and his cargo. Jen wasn't sure if they were acting or if they really couldn't see them.

He had tossed the other two girls on the bed and joined them. She tried not to listen from her place on the floor, but her hearing was unfortunately still very clear. She heard the girls try to cry for help, but they could only whisper, and that was incoherent. She heard other sounds and tried to find a happy place in her mind.

After a few minutes, he came down off the bed and picked her up, propping her against the bed. He leaned against the bed casually and smiled at her.

"I wonder about you," he said.

Jen gave him a look that made him pause.

"Whoa," he said, laughing. "What was that?? Jiminy, come in here please?"

The cricket jumped into the room, swiveled, and leaped to the young man's shoulder. He tossed his hair casually and gestured at Jen. "Loosen her up a little. I wanna chat."

The cricket chirped.

"Just enough so she can talk. Not enough to move."

The cricket leapt onto Jen's leg. She twitched, and then turned her head to look directly at the young man.

The cricket chirped.

"Well she did move her head, but I think she's ok. Just don't do any more." He shoved one of the girls over and sat down on the bed.

"So... you aren't like these two. Why are you hanging with them?"

Jen glared at the young man. Her jaw worked and she looked like she was ready to kill him.

"My little buddy loosened you up, so I know you can-"

"Yes, I can talk. I just have nothing to say to you."

Chapter Sixteen

Trapped inside her sphere, Serena could hear what Dorian was saying, even if it was huge, deep, and muffled.

"If you tell me where they are, I swear to unSphere you and let you and your friend go," he said. "I swear it on the Oath."

This was serious. Even DaiUi didn't swear on the Oath unless they intended to do whatever it was they were swearing. Swearing on the Oath meant you were promising to the Others that you would do it. If you swore on the Oath and then broke your vow, you were putting yourself in jeopardy of being Severed by the Others. No one wanted that. Even the Dark One herself feared being Severed.

Serena didn't understand why Dorian was doing these things, but she gathered from the way Eric had looked at him that Dorian wasn't who he appeared to be. Or maybe When he appeared to be.

"Where who is," Serena said in a flat tone.

"Strode and Alisha. Tell me where they went and I'll let you two go free. We'll walk out and you won't see us again."

"Are you really Dorian?" asked Serena with a little more inflection.

"Yes. I'm Dorian many, many centuries from now," said future Dorian.

"So you join the DaiUi?"

Dorian just looked at her Sphere. She couldn't see him, but she felt the withering gaze that Dorian used when people asked stupid questions.

"I guess that answers my question," she muttered, mostly to herself.

"Where are they??" Dorian asked very loudly. He almost never lost his patience, so this was a little unsettling. Serena wondered how much people's personalities shifted when they joined the DaiUi. She guessed it was different for everyone.

"Fortunately for me, and for Strode, Alisha, and Eric, all I can tell you is exactly all I WOULD tell you even if I COULD tell you more," said Serena.

"You don't know," guessed Dorian, somewhat accurately.

"Are you going to let me answer you, or should I just let you guess all of my responses?" asked Serena with her customary sarcasm.

Dorian just waited.

"They went sweeping. I have no idea when or where they are now. Even if I knew what year they started in, which I don't-"

"OK, I get it. You're useless. But you told me all you know, and I gave you my word," said future Dorian.

The next thing Serena knew, she was rolling onto her feet in the room, seeing Eric do the same a few feet away, and they were the only ones left in the room.

Chapter Seventeen

The young man tossed his hair again, but with a curious look. He looked at Jen with a mixture of "bored, been there done that" cynicism and genuine curiosity. The curiosity was beginning to win out.

"So why do you hang out with these two, when you're so obviously not like them?"

Jen looked at the man straight in the eyes for a long time, then looked away.

"If you tell me why you hang out with them, I'll let one of them go," he said, measuredly.

"Sure you will," she said.

"No, I will. You have my word."

Jen puffed out a huge breath of incredulous laughter. "Your word. You drug and rape my friends, drug me and will probably kill all three of us, and I'm supposed to think you have some kind of honor??"

"You know I do."

Jen looked hard at him. She bore holes in his eyes with hers. "You will. I don't know how, but you actually plan to let us go."

"I plan to let THEM go. I have other plans for you."

Chapter Eighteen

And on the seventh sweep of the usual suspects in the year 1745...
Strode and Alisha found him.

With seventeen other Spheres, he was floating in a section of space
between two asteroids near Ceres, the dwarf planet in the Solar
System between Mars and Jupiter. The Ui were unsure why the
DaiUi kept Spheres here, and in a few decades the Dark One realized
that the Ui had discovered them there and they then move them to a
currently unknown location. But until they do, the Ui travel back to
that time and often find Spheres there.

Strode and Isha weren't sure who they found, only that they had
discovered eighteen Spheres floating in space. They collected the
Spheres and brought them back to Sri Kaǎsala. It was easier to travel
with them Sphered. When they entered the Ui discussion room, they
placed the Spheres on cushions on the floor and unSphered them.

They discovered sixteen Ui who had been lost for several years.
They also discovered Aka Atachi, who had been communicating
with the other Atachis the entire time, and taking part in their work
and adventures, but couldn't tell them where he was since he himself
didn't know. His reunion was happy, but not too rambunctious since
he'd been with them all along in everything except body. But his
body was happy to be free of that Sphere and out running around
again.

But the 18th member to be freed was David. David had been lost to
the Ui for almost a century. He must have been shuffled to that
location "recently" because they'd swept that area many times and
never found him before. Somehow they caught him after he'd been
transferred there, but before he'd been relocated to the new DaiUi
location.

In any case, he was in good shape and peaceful, but very quiet. The
unSphering was done gently, as you never knew the condition of the
person in the Sphere. David was sitting in the lotus position inside
his Sphere, and he dropped a few inches onto the cushion. He

opened his eyes slowly, and looked at everyone expressionlessly. He very slightly and slowly nodded to Strode. Then he saw Alisha, and his face slowly transformed.

He frowned. Then his eyes welled up with tears, but they never fell. The corners of his mouth turned up, and it was hard to tell if it was a smile or a painful grimace or both. Given his and Isha's history, it was probably both.

For Isha's part, she ugly cried. She sobbed like a baby and wrapped her arms around his neck and hung on like her life depended on it. Maybe it did.

Chapter Nineteen

Amon moved a pawn. Even though he'd just spent close to an hour studying the board and thinking a dozen moves ahead, he was still worried he was making a terrible mistake. The girl across the board from him looked like she was about ten years old. He knew she was much, much older than that. Or maybe she wasn't. She had been alive for many, many years. For some reason the Ui seemed reluctant to specify how old they were. And it might just be that age was not a constant like he formerly thought.

What is age, after all? he asked himself. If it is how long we've lived, determining how long we have LEFT to live, and indicating how much "age" our bodies should show, then age was nonexistent among the Ui. No matter how long they'd lived, they would continue to live as long as they chose to. Conceivably, they would never die. And they didn't grow old... their bodies showed no signs of "age". So it could be said that it was, in fact, entirely irrelevant how many years had transpired since they were born.

Especially when you took into account the fact that they had all time traveled. If Amy, the girl who was currently trouncing him in chess, was born 500 years ago, but had traveled back in time 1,000 times, and each time waited until the current time to then go back 2,000 years, how "old" was she now? That's a word problem he was glad he didn't have to solve.

However long Amy had "been around", millions of years she said, but never how many exactly, she clearly had mastered chess along the way. There were very few people who could ever beat her, and no one could do it consistently. What she didn't tell Amon was that she had mastered chess very early. She had only played Oko a couple hundred times before she began beating him, game after game. This was, of course, "before" Oko became one of the DaiUi. And before Amy beat him, he was the best chess player anyone knew. (He didn't leave the Ui because Amy beat him. In case you were wondering.)

Amon wasn't sure why Amy asked him to play. He knew that

beating him game after game after game had to be excruciatingly boring for her. But she never acted like it. Granted, she was reading a book and composing a symphony at the same time she was playing him. But her face seemed genuinely interested in the game for the few seconds she took to study the board before making her perfect, indefensible, inscrutable moves. Amon was a great chess player back home. But he was fairly certain he would never, ever come close to beating Amy.

In the center of the room, Dorian, David, Alisha, Eric, and Serena were debriefing. During the next couple of weeks, David would meet with all of the members of the Ui and get their reflections and information on what had happened in his absence. But it was important that Dorian, Eric, and Serena bring David up to speed on what happened most recently. Dorian was at a loss why he had returned from the future to try to find Alisha and Strode.

David looked at Dorian for a long time, weighing things. "I don't know what that means, either," he said finally in a weak and quiet voice. "It seems as though you will join the DaiUi in the future. Whether you genuinely join or whether we send you as spy or something else we don't even know, will remain to be seen. For now, I can only assume that you're telling us the truth and are not currently spying for the DaiUi or have any plans to join them." He looked at Dorian with a question in his eyes.

"I don't know how to tell you anything you don't already know," said Dorian. "Anything I say will be precisely what I would say if I were trying to convince you, even though I was lying. All I can say is, I swear on the Oath that I am not spying, that I have no intention of joining the DaiUi, and that I'm fully committed to the Ui."

"That's all we can ask," said David weakly, obviously making up his mind on the matter. "So why do you think you were looking for Strode and Isha?"

"I've been thinking about it," said Dorian. "But I have no idea."

"Strode? Isha? Any thoughts? Eric and Serena?"

"I don't know if there's any way for us to know why he was looking for us other than to ask him," said Alisha. "Why don't we send a team forward and find out?"

David looked dubious. "I don't know if we want to risk that just now. Let's spend some time with the seventeen people we brought back today, get them re-acclimated... and figure out our strategy if we do send a team to find out. Or if you come back. We also need to figure out how you and your guys got past the security perimeter," he said, looking at Dorian. "I'm hoping for the spy scenario."

"Me too," said Dorian gloomily.

Amon set the board up for another game with Amy. While reading Finnegans Wake and composing her third symphony of the day, she was obliterating him over and over on the chessboard while answering his questions.

"Why don't you bring people here, where it's safe, and explain how it all works before you have them Drink? Seems like that would cause there to be fewer who leave?" he asked as he moved a knight.

"Do you know when we are?" Amy asked, touching the table to her left in various places, to alternating rhythms. Finnegans Wake was scrolling quickly on a virtual screen to her right. She watched the words scroll by as she touched the table.

"Maria said we were in the first century CE," said Amon.

"Yes, we keep Sri Kaąsala, now, starting 500 years before Christ and we're currently in 93AD," said Amy. She watched the words closely and tapped the table in a complicated way, frowning slightly.

".... are you putting Finnegans Wake to music?" asked Amon incredulously.

"I'm trying to. If I get it right, it'll be a nice loop," she said. "So if we bring someone to Sri Kaąsala who happens to live between 500 BC and 93AD, then we could bring them here, though we'd have to create a physical door, among other things."

"They couldn't just come through the fountain?"

"Their body could. But they wouldn't survive the trip. And of course they wouldn't survive the journey from any other time, either," she explained.

"How many times have you explained this?" asked Amon.

"To you? Three," she said, and her eyes danced as she watched the words. This was the closest Amy ever came to smiling.

"No, I mean..." he fumbled, turning red. "How many times have you taught people this same information?"

"This will be my 739th time," she said simply.

"Doesn't it get old, repeating the same words over and over?" he asked.

"It might if I were talking to a wall. But people make it interesting. They ask different questions, wonder about different things. They take delight in aspects that I never considered. If I got bored, which we never do, I would just ask questions back. People are fascinating."

"So you have to take the people, while they're still mortal, to the pool in Florida? Are there any other pools?"

"There are supposed to be seven pools. But we don't know how many, if any, of the other pools are extant. We've been looking for them."

"Do the other pools have snakes and fruit, too?"

"That's what they say."

Eric and Strode started a competition.

"There's no way you can beat me," said Eric.

"We'll see," said Strode.

"What's the bet?" asked Serena.

"Eric thinks he can make Amy smile before I can," said Strode, frowning.

"Can I get in on this?" asked Serena.

"Sure you can. You think I can do it first, right?" asked Eric.

"I'll bet whatever you guys want that neither of you will be able to get her to smile," said Serena.

"We each get a Xlix," said Strode.

"If what?" asked Serena.

"If either of us get her to smile," said Eric.

"Done," said Serena.

Eric and Strode both looked at Amy. She went on building her symphony and schooling Amon in chess and other things.

"So," asked Amon, "I know that I had to eat the fruit and drink the … liquid... before going down into the fountain and having the dagger stabbed into my heart. But I still don't understand the fruits. How many are there again? Why can't we eat more than one? What do they do?"

Amy continued watching the words to Finnegans Wake scroll up the screen while tapping on the table in alternating rhythms. She would occasionally frown and hit some kind of reset on the side of the table, and then redo what she had just done in a different way. Amon could feel the method in the midst of her madness, but just barely.

"The fruits grow only on that tree, and that's the only one of those trees that we have found so far. There are supposed to be six more pools, and we have heard that each one has a tree, maybe more kinds of trees, too, at each pool. We have been searching longer than you can imagine to try to find another pool, hoping to find more fruit and maybe other types of trees that do who knows what?" she paused, seemingly for breath, and Amon processed what she was saying while desperately trying to find a chink in her chess armor.

"You are only supposed to eat one, because while it provides what you need to internally fortify and externally protect your body for the coming transformation in the fountain, it does so using only one fruit. As long as you use the juice mixed into the fluid in the goblet. But since the tree doesn't produce any more fruit, we are limited to only producing as many Ui as there are fruits on that tree. If anyone eats more than one, that's one fewer Ui that we can transform."

Chapter Twenty

The young man looked at Jen. She glared back at him.

"Why do I feel like you always have the upper hand?" he asked.

She looked him in the eye, then looked at the white ring around his neck. It was about the thickness of a wedding band, but long enough to easily fit around the biggest neck. It was solid white, and looked like stone, though it was actually metal.

"You wonder about my ring?"

She stared at it for a long time. Then she looked him in the eye and said, "I'm going to take that from you."

He laughed. "You've got nerve, I'll give you that. But you have no idea who you're dealing with, or even WHAT you're dealing with. I could crush you into a tiny ball with one hand without even thinking about it."

She looked at him levelly, and knew he wouldn't. Couldn't.

"But I've got other plans for you," he said, fighting off the nervousness that suddenly crept into his bones. He got up, touched the two girls on the bed on their feet, and they relaxed into unconsciousness. He put their robes back on them, carried them out to the hot tub, and sat them down on the deck chairs. While he was gone, Jen tried desperately to move, tried to run. She could barely move her eyes. The frustration was enough to crush her, but she bit it down and concentrated.

He came back into the room and picked her up, put her on the bed, and sat down on the chair next to the bed.

"You probably think we should get out of here, that they're going to wake up and go tell the cops what happened. But they won't remember anything. They'll be sore tomorrow, but they won't remember why. It'll haunt them for a while, but you'd be surprised how quickly people come up with other explanations for things... try to make them make sense in their own heads. Before long they'll forget they were even here."

Chapter Twenty-One

Alisha and David on the floor, staring at the ceiling in the fountain room. They had been talking, sat down after a dozen hours, then both reclined on their elbow... finally just laid back and grew quiet.

They listened to the fountain splashing.

They could barely make out the sound of the other one breathing.

David's hand moved over and touched the side of Alisha's hand, stayed there. Their minds were lost in the time they'd spent apart... and then time before that. Just in the simple touch of one finger against another, they experienced the connection that they'd been missing for over a hundred years.

Eternities passed.

Chapter Twenty-two

"OK. I've given you a token of good faith. I've let them both go, without you doing anything for me at all. So now tell me, why were you with them?"

Jen swallowed. She looked around the room. "Give me some water and I'll tell you."

The young man got up, filled a glass with water, and held it up to her mouth. She drank, and a little water ran down her chin. He grabbed a towel and dried it.

He sat down and waited.

Jen cleared her throat. She looked at the window, where the blinds were drawn closed, and said, "I knew them from when we were … we grew up together. We've been friends for as long as I can remember."

He waited.

"We were really good friends when we were young, and did everything together. We planned... anyway. As we grew up, they got closer and I became the odd girl out. They started hanging out with this guy named Ja-, with this guy. He got them into drugs and drinking all the time and then they all three started sleeping together. It really hurt me, because they were my best friends. I felt like they betrayed me." Jen seemed to remember that he was in the room and her face grew cold.

"Anyway, that's why we were together. They were my friends. I care about them. They're making horrible decisions, and it almost cost them their lives tonight. From what you've said, it DID cost me mine."

"Just the opposite, little one," said the young man. "Because of them, you will never die."

Chapter Twenty-three

David and Alisha, Strode and Serena, Eric and Amy all sat around the conference table in the discussion room. They were discussing Dorian, and Dorian had excused himself so they could speak candidly without the distraction of his presence and his feelings to hamper their objective decisions.

"So does anyone feel like Dorian is currently our enemy?" asked Strode.

Everyone shook their head except Amy. She stared into the space above their heads and frowned slightly. She was considering all of her interactions with Dorian, and weighing each of them against her trust in him. Everyone else had done the same thing, but Amy took these things to heart. She felt like it was her responsibility to keep the group unemotional and objective in their decisions, because she had known every other member to make their choices based too much on their feelings and not enough on the facts at hand. While she respected David's wisdom and leadership, she felt that he sometimes put his feelings before his wisdom in his decision making. Particularly where Alisha was concerned. But she'd seen it in his decisions with all of them. He would always err on the side of protecting his people, and Amy preferred not to err at all.

"I don't remember him acting in any particularly dubious ways," she said. "And all of his choices reflect a deep commitment to the group. If he's spying on us now, he's the best spy I've ever known."

Everyone nodded and a couple murmured their agreement. This was tantamount to saying that Dorian was above reproach.

Chapter Twenty-four

The young man picked up Jen and carried her to the door. "I can walk," she said.

He put her down and gave her a look. "I can trust you not to run off?"

"If I try to run, your little friend will just immobilize me again," she said, clearly meaning it.

He looked at her for a few more seconds. "What if you scream? Yell for help?"

"I can only assume that you will drug me and kill them. The only way I can prevent other people from being hurt is to cooperate," she said dully, robotically, in a flat tone.

"One other thing. You might notice that no one else did. Notice, I mean. People don't notice me or what I'm doing. It's something I've set up that causes people to ignore me. Once you learn what I am, what's different about me, I'll explain more. But for now, just know that no one will see you or hear you if you try to ask for help. You WILL, as you said, just get them hurt."

She looked at him when he said "what I am", her eyes a little bigger than normal. She nodded.

"OK then."

He gestured to the door. She pulled her robe around her in a dignified way and walked to the door. "I'd like some actual clothes. And I wanna know where you're taking me."

"Sure, I can get you some clothes. That's reasonable. And I'll tell you this – we're going to Florida."

"What's in Florida?"

"You'll see when we get there."

"Why don't you just-"

"That's enough for now. Go get in the car, don't make any fuss, and I'll trust you to keep you mobilized. If you try anything, I won't just immobilize you. I'll hurt you."

She looked at him, then away. She nodded.

They went out and got in the car like nothing was odd about the whole thing. The cricket rode on the young man's shoulder.

He pulled out of the hotel parking lot and into traffic.

"I'm surprised you haven't asked me my name yet," he said.

"I don't care what your name is," she said.

"Fair enough."

The young man drove for seventeen hours straight, stopping only to get gas. Jen used the restroom and grabbed junk food at each gas station. He never seemed to eat or sleep or use the restroom.

"Aren't you curious why I never do any of those things?" asked the man.

"I don't use this word lightly. I really mean it. I LITERALLY could not care less," said Jen.

The man looked at her and smiled slightly. "The less you are curious about me, the more I'm intrigued by you," he said.

She looked out the window and sighed.

In six more hours, they crossed the state line into Florida. They stopped at the first gas station they came to. The man filled the tank while Jen went in to the gas station store.

She went straight to the bathrooms and stood in the short line. The girl in line ahead of her turned around like she knew Jen, frowned, and looked at the floor for a second. Then she nodded and looked back at Jen. The other two girls in line had headphones on and tunes cranked, and no one else was around.

"My name is Sheila and I know you're in trouble," she said, looking Jen in the eye and then looking back at the floor casually.

"What? How d-… no, I'm not. What are you talking about?" Jen stammered, shocked out of her determination to act normal.

"It's OK. I'm on your side. I know you're in trouble and I can help you," she said, looking at the floor.

"I .. don't know what you mean. I'm just here to use the bathroom and get gas," Jen looked at the door to the bathroom and wished the line would just friggin' MOVE.

"I know you can't talk about it. I know he's threatened to hurt anyone who you talk to. I don't know what he's going to do to you, but I know it's not good. Here's my card. It says it's for a business opportunity, so he won't know what it's about if he finds it. Just put it in your pocket. When the time is right, call me. We will send someone to help you. I know what he can do," she said this emphatically, and looked Jen in the eye when she said it, "And don't worry. We can handle him. Call me."

She pressed the card into Jen's palm and left the line, went to the front of the store, bought a drink, and left.

Jen's heart was racing. She looked at the card. It had a name "Stephanie Burrell" and the words "exciting business opportunity" across the top. There was a number on the bottom of the card, but it had too many numbers in it to be a phone number. Jen wondered if the whole thing was a trick by the young man to see what she would do. But something in "Stephanie"'s tone told her it wasn't. She sensed on some deep level that she could trust her, that she would do what she said. She stuck the card in her pocket.

Chapter Twenty-Five

Amon moved his rook three spaces over, and felt like he might actually be forming a strategy that could work against Amy's truly intimidating onslaught on the chessboard. She listened to her Finnegans Wake symphony and glanced at the board for two seconds, moved a pawn, and devastated any hope he had of winning the game.

"So tell me again why we're not wasting time here? We are, and correct me if I'm wrong, because I'm still trying to … how do you say? Wrap my brain around? The idea of who we are exactly. So … we are immortal time travelers who can do pretty much anything we want. But instead of solving world hunger or saving the Jews from Auschwitz, we are sitting around playing chess, composing symphonies, rescuing our own members from their own stupidity, and basically … what looks like wasting our time??" Amon ran out of steam.

"Wasting our what?" asked Amy, starting a new symphony while scrolling the Divine Comedy.

"TI-!..... oh." said Amon.

Amy let it sink in.

"Tell me what you just realized," said Amy in what would have been a patient tone from anyone else. From Amy it was just... Amy.

"We can't waste time. It's... not possible. We have an infinite amount of time. No matter how long it takes us to go back and fix things, or go forward and fix things, it'll still be there … when we go. We can't run out of time because we can't ever run out of time, literally."

"And?" she asked.

"And... so... it's important for us to train. And think. And train more. So that when we DO go back... or forward... we're ready."

"Yes... but why do we play music and write poems and play tennis and fall in love?"

"Because... because these things make living worth living?"

"You're getting warmer," she said, her eyes dancing a little.

"Because we are preserving something?"

"That's part of it, yes. Keep going," she tapped on the table in an unusual rhythm.

"Because it... it keeps us human?"

"It does. What else? You're missing the most important reason."

Amon thought about the chess game for a while, and mulled it over.

Chapter Twenty-six

They drove across Florida. At the next gas station, Jen went in to use the bathroom and get a drink. She took the card out in the bathroom and looked at it. It had the name Stephanie Burrell and a number. She didn't recognize the area code, but she wasn't sure what Florida area codes looked like. She thought about calling the number, but she was afraid of so many things. Mostly she was afraid that she would drag some poor woman into her situation and get her killed. She hadn't seen the young man kill anyone yet, but she could tell he would, without hesitation or mercy. And she didn't even want to think about that cricket.

She put the card back in her pocket, bought a drink, and went back out to the car.

To say that things would have been different if she had called the number is an enormous understatement.

It was the last mistake she made before her death.

Chapter Twenty-seven

Amon looked up. "Is it because …. because fixing things isn't the most important part of life?"

Amy glanced at him. "Go on..."

"Well... of course there are horrible things in the world. And it's definitely our responsibility to do what we can to fix them. Right?"

"Yes," she said.

"But the most important thing in life isn't to fix the problems that others are causing. We aren't just supposed to be reacting to evil, we should be... it's more important that we .. that we DO something for GOOD."

"Like what?"

"Like create beautiful music. Paint amazing art. Enjoy life, have fun together, LIVE LIFE!" he said, getting a little carried away with his own thought.

"That's the beginning," she said, and her eyes danced, just a little.

Chapter Twenty-eight

The young man carried Jen, now once again paralyzed, into the fountain. He propped her against the side so she wouldn't drown just yet. He reached up and plucked a fruit from the tree growing nearby. Squeezing it, he poured the juice into her mouth, which he also squeezed to open. He could see the mix of hate, fear, and struggle in her eyes. But she was unable to do anything in defense. He swam down into the fountain and returned with a goblet. He lifted it, dripping, from the fountain, full of liquid. He lifted it to her lips and again forced her to drink.

Then he pulled her down into the fountain and she felt the liquid close above her head. She could do nothing but succumb. He pulled a stone dagger out of his waistband and the last thing she remembered in this life was him plunging the dagger into her heart.

Chapter Twenty-nine

David climbed out of the sens-dep chamber pulling his robe on. He touched the button on the side of Alisha's unit that let her know through a very quiet tone that she was being requested outside of her chamber. In a few seconds her door popped open a crack and her hand reached out. David put her robe into her hand and then walked around to the other side of her chamber. She climbed out, pulling on her robe, and joined him where he was standing.

"Feeling yourself again?" she asked.

"Getting there," he said quietly, hoarsely. He hadn't talked much since he emerged from his Sphere. Verbal communication was a difficult habit to get used to when in solitude for as long as he'd been.

He flashed her a message in their mental link. 'Thanks for being patient with me.'

'No problem. Take as long as you need,' she flashed back.

'I should probably eat something,' he shot to her.

'Are you hungry?' she asked, then grimaced. 'Sorry, forget I asked that.'

He looked at her with a blank expression, but his eyes were talking. 'It's ok. Don't feel like you have to break your conversational habits just because I'm still getting up to speed.'

'I'm still not used to your face being so blank,' she sent him, bluntly.

'Is it? I feel like I'm being expressive. I guess I've got more recovery left than I thought.'

'What do you feel like eating?'

'Something small. And fluidish.'

'A fruit smoothie?'

'Perfect.'

They left the sens-dep room and walked down the hall to the kitchen. Alisha made them some smoothies while David sifted through messages on his internal mail system. His body sat down on the floor and assumed the lotus.

'Is that comfortable, even after all this time?' Alisha wanted to know.

'Is what.. oh. I didn't even realize I was doing it. My body just does this automatically when I'm lost in thought. I was checking my messages.'

'Anything interesting?'

'Yes, actually. We may have a lead on where number two is.'

Chapter Thirty

Amon watched Amy finish tapping on the little stone table. She listened for a few seconds, her head tilted and her eyes closed. Then she nodded.

"Can I hear it?" he asked.

She looked at him seriously for a few seconds, as though weighing him with her eyes. Then she nodded very slightly, one time.

She touched something on the table and suddenly Amon could hear a tiny sound stirring somewhere in the remote distance. It slowly grew in volume. He looked around the room and noticed that no one else seemed to hear the sound. They were all continuing their conversations like normal.

Amy sent him a direct message. 'Only you can hear this. It's being sent directly to your tympanic cells. It can be as loud or as soft as you desire. Just think about the volume getting louder or softer and it'll respond.'

He turned it up.

Chapter Thirty-one

Jen woke up.

She was sure that she … she died. She remembered feeling the waves close over her head, felt the thrust of the stone knife into her heart. There's no way she could have survived that.

She was lying on a grassy area, her head propped up on a cushion. She was wearing a white robe. She was alone.

She looked around and saw only grass and trees and sunshine and clouds as far as she could see. It was warm, but there was a gentle, pleasant breeze.

For the first time in... well, for the first time ever, she didn't know where she was. She didn't know how she got there. She wasn't even sure who she was. She would have been useless in an interview.

Her hands went to her chest, but she didn't feel any wound where the dagger had … had done its work. She didn't even feel a scar, or a line, or anything. In fact, her chest felt better than it had in years. Maybe better than it ever had. She suddenly realized that her senses were different... she could hear everything. She could focus on a tree, and hear the wind as it ruffled the leaves, hear the wood creak and groan as it moved ever so slightly. She could hear the grass growing. It was a whispery, almost papery sound coming from all around her at once. She wasn't sure why her hearing impressed itself on her so suddenly. Especially since she could also see everything.

She could look at a single blade of grass on the hill behind three hills in front of her. She could see tiny bugs crawling on that blade of grass. She could see bugs crawling on that bug. She lost interest in the bugs when she remembered that she wasn't breathing.

She wasn't breathing.

She didn't notice at first. It was something she took for granted all her life. But she was just resting on the grass, feeling and hearing and seeing everything. And not breathing.

She drew in a breath. It worked fine. She blew it out. No problem. So she COULD breathe. But she apparently didn't need to. She stopped breathing and waited. She kept thinking that any minute now she would start feeling that burning in her lungs telling her to take a breath. She sensed that SOMETHING was happening inside her, where her respiration took place. But she didn't need air.

She got up and stretched. She didn't feel stiff or sore. She felt... amazing. She felt very alive. Very healthy. She felt better than she could ever remember feeling ever before. She felt... perfect.

Chapter Thirty-two

'Who knows where number two is?' asked Alisha eagerly.

'They're not sure, but Strode and Serena have a lead. They found a cluster of Spheres near Land's End in 1287. They're having trouble getting close, though... it's a well-protected cluster.'

Alisha looked at him pointedly.

'I don't think it's a good idea to send you out again so soon. It wasn't even wise for you to go looking for me... but I know there was no way anyone could have stopped you.'

'Short of Sphering me,' she half joked.

David looked at her. They held a conversation about the subject of her being Sphered for several minutes without sending even mental words. They talked with their eyes, sort of like old married couples do, but to the nth degree. They were thousands of years past old married couples.

Challenges, acquiesces, questions, pleas, and apologies flowed back and forth between them without the need of cumbersome words.

'Then who DO we send?' she asked finally.

'How far along is Amon?'

Alisha looked at him sharply.

'He's only been training for a few weeks.'

'How are he and Amy getting along?'

'Perfectly. I think he's getting over his feelings that he owes her,' she said.

'Any romantic feelings developing?'

'Not that we can tell. He still thinks of her as a little girl,' she observed.

'It does usually take a while for people to get past that. What are the cool kids doing?'

'They're still dealing with the DaiUi trouble in Miramar.'

'Still?'

'Yes. They had it contained and were headed back when another group returned to the same time and caused more mayhem. They've almost got it done but it'll take a little more time.'

'Can we send the Atachis?'

'I wondered why you didn't ask about them first.'

'They're a good choice, of course. I just wanted to give them a little more Rest and Strategize time before we sent them back out.'

'Normally I would agree, but we might need to check out this Sphere cluster before it gets shuffled again.'

'Can you let them know?'

'I'll ask Amy to let them know. I think they still resent me.'

'Good plan.'

Alisha looked at him closely. 'How are you feeling?'

'I'm fine. A little slow still, physically. I didn't have any slowing mentally, and I spent most of my Sphered time with the Others, so spiritually I'm tip top. I just have to get my body used to movement again. Even talking is exhausting right now.'

'I'll let you get some rest,' she started to leave.

'Please come back after you tell Amy.'

Alisha flushed, smiled shyly, and nodded. She went out.

Chapter Thirty-three

Jen wandered around and pretty much just found more grass. She came across an occasional tree, but no fauna. The sun never moved from its spot in the sky. She thought maybe she was just experiencing a long "moment" at first, but when she had been there for a while, she realized that it wasn't moving. With no sun movement, and nothing but grass and trees, she wasn't sure how long she was there. She had no way of gauging time. She never felt hungry or thirsty or tired. Her muscles never grew tired, no matter what position she was in or how long she stayed like that. She tried it, to be sure. She stood on one hand and lifted her entire body up into the air, not even bothering to balance. She was able to hold up her entire body with one hand, at an angle, for as long as she wanted. She wasn't even sure how the physics of that worked. It seemed like sheer gravity would pull her down. If she was a statue built at that angle, she would fall over. But she could hold herself like that indefinitely.

She had just about decided that she was in some kind of boring heaven when she saw them.

Chapter Thirty-four

Amon ran. He struggled to keep up with Amy. She was running easily ahead of him, moving with such ease and grace that it boggled his brain. They were in a forest outside of Prague. She had taken him out through the fountain. They emerged in Florida in 2044. They flew from Florida to Prague, and then started running. Amon wasn't sure what this part of the training was until he saw Amy run. She moved so fast, so agilely, so smoothly and with every movement counting that it was clear he needed to work on his form.

He could already run faster than he could have ever imagined. He ran faster than the fastest plane he'd heard of. At first just keeping track of what was coming and avoiding objects took up all of his attention. But then his brain acclimated, and he adapted to his terrain without even paying attention. He could focus on other things. Like working on his form. He thought he was getting pretty good at moving with focused, controlled movements until he saw Amy run.

Amy ran like the wind. She flowed over the countryside almost faster than he could watch, let alone follow. He tried to focus on losing unnecessary movements and concentrate all of his energy on a better running form. The distance between him and Amy grew larger. He relaxed and thought about getting where he was going faster. His body responded and the distance to Amy lessened. He wasn't sure if she was letting him catch up or not, but he did sense that he was going faster now.

Amon realized that he was learning to RUN, of all things. You would think that he would have mastered running when he was about five years old. Or at the latest, in his teens when he ran track in school. But he was actually learning something as simple as running, and learning all over again how to do it better than ever before.

So he began to realize that he would have to relearn... everything.

He called up to her, and found that he could talk to her just as though they were in the same room standing still. Even though they were running faster than a plane flies. He wasn't sure about the physics of this, but he wasn't worried about that now. He was thinking about the Spheres.

"So tell me again how the Ui can't get out of the Spheres?" he asked.

"When you're Sphered, the Sphere moves when you move. So you can't ever get to the edge of the Sphere to break out." She said without slowing.

That made sense. But he wondered something else. "Didn't you say that you can change the way time moves?"

"Not exactly. We can change the way we experience time. Just like we're able to move so fast that mortals can't see us. If we keep moving and thinking that fast, then time seems much slower. We can accomplish millions of things and think billions of thoughts in the space of microseconds. But we can also do the opposite. We can move so slowly, and think so slowly, that time seems to speed up. Then it could take a thousand years for me to count to ten."

"Why would you want that?"

"Can't you think of a time when you would want time to go faster?"

He thought about it.

"If I was doing something I didn't want to do. Like if I was stuck somewhere and couldn't leave."

"Like when you're…." she prompted.

"Oh. Like when I'm Sphered."

She nodded seriously.

"So we can just make time do this at will?"

"We're not changing time. We're changing the way we experience it by speeding ourselves up or slowing ourselves down."

"How do you learn to do this?"

"We learn going faster by practice. It's not hard. You just start doing whatever you're doing faster and faster, and you find you can do it and you can keep track of everything and it's not hard. Until you get going at the top speed that Ui can do things. It's hard to explain how fast that is, but once you've started doing it the nomenclature will make more sense and I'll tell you how to gauge it."

"How do you learn to go more slowly?"

"By spending time with the Others."

Chapter Thirty-five

Jen walked across the clearing between two copses of trees. As she did, she thought to herself that the word "copse" means "a small group of trees". So "a copse of trees" is redundant. She should just say "I'm walking between two copses." But she knew that if she said that, people would be confused. Sometimes redundancy is good for emphasis. And other times for clarification.

She wondered why she was thinking such pedantic and technical things, and wondered if maybe her brain was doing that thing that human brains do when they're frightened by something huge and other. When something outside of their comfortable little lives looms threateningly, human brains latch on to the familiar and the small in order to cope. In order to keep from being freaked out completely. And she was certainly coming across something unfamiliar now.

As she walked between the copses, she felt herself dreading going any farther. She saw three... people? Walking toward her. They were definitely human looking. But there was something about them that... transcended humanity. She wasn't sure what she even meant by that, if anything. But she knew that she was coming face to … face with beings she never even knew existed, let alone had talked to before. And fear of the unknown can be one mind-stultifying fear.

It wasn't just fear of the unknown, though, she realized. How she was making all of these realizations in the short time it took to walk to these … people and talk to them, she wasn't sure. But it was almost as though time were changing around her as she walked. Fear will do that, too, she knew. But this was something else. THEY were something else. She was very afraid of them.

While her fear and... awe were growing, she realized that these feelings came with a sense of … ancient familiarity. It wasn't exactly that she didn't know who she was about to face. It was that, way back deep in the recesses of her mind, way back in the part of her inherited consciousness, she DID know who they were. They were the Others. And she had known them all along.

Chapter Thirty-six

Amy stopped. Amon was, of course, not ready for this, and he zoomed by her going so fast that he didn't realize where she went at first. She just vanished.

He slowed and stopped. He looked around. Finally he looked behind him and saw her several miles back. He ran back to her and stopped, looking at the ground where she was looking.

There was blood on the ground.

Chapter Thirty-seven

Alisha sent Amy a message. 'I need you to talk to the Atachis for me.'

Amy looked at the blood. 'Can you get someone else? I'm in the middle of something.'

Alisha's eyes widened slightly and her eyebrows elevated. Amy had never said anything like this before. She was always dutiful, to a fault. She erred on the side of accepting way too much responsibility, way too many tasks. For her to demur meant that something huge was happening.

'Uh, sure. No problem. You ok?' Alisha asked.

'Yes, I'm fine. I'll get back to you.'

Alisha shot David this, 'Amy begged off. Who would you like me to ask? Dorian?'

A pause. She sensed him mulling it over. Finally, 'Sure.'

Alisha messaged Dorian 'Where you at?'

She waited. Listened in while David's internal monologue leaked over into an external hum. Smiled at John. "He doesn't know I can hear that," she said out loud.

John smiled back "You should tell him."

"I will," she grinned mischievously. "Eventually."

John was Isha's friend, and only Isha could see or hear him. This will make more sense later in the story.

Chapter Thirty-eight

Amon looked at the red spot quizzically. "Do you think this is from an animal?"

Amy seemed to stare through the red splotches and into the depths of the earth. She always looked very serious. Amon had never seen her smile, laugh, cry, or give any overt sign of emotion besides her occasional dancing eyes. As she stared into the bloodstain, though, he thought he saw something new.

Amy crouched and touched her forefinger to the redness. She lifted it, examined her finger thoughtfully, and looked off vaguely north, to the left of the direction in which they'd been running.

"It called to me," she said.

"The animal?" he asked, listening hard.

"No. The blood."

Amon looked at her, then off into the distance in which she was transfixed. "What did it say?"

"It wasn't words. It cried to me, for me to find out what happened and to make things right."

"So how are you going to do that?" Amon wasn't sure if she was speaking literally or metaphorically, and he definitely wasn't going to ask. Some questions didn't deserve to be asked.

"First I have to go that way, and find the source of this blood. It's from a young woman, and she's in immediate danger. Mortal danger." She looked at the blood again.

"You can tell all that from looking?" he looked at her finger. Definitely red.

"Not just looking. I'm analyzing the chemical content of the blood.

There are hormones and acids in the blood that the body only produces when the person is in extreme stress or agony. This blood has them. She needs my help." So probably literally. With a splash of metaphor.

"OK, then let's go."

She looked at Amon, and he couldn't help but feel patronized. She seemed to size up him and the situation and then she nodded. "OK, just stay with me and don't hesitate if I ask you to do something."

He looked at her, a little alarmed. Then he thought back to the time he'd spent with her already, and the wisdom and compassion she'd already demonstrated so profoundly. He knew he could trust her.

"OK. I won't."

"Then let's go." She ran off in the direction they'd been looking, even faster than before. This time, for some reason, Amon had little trouble keeping up.

Chapter Thirty-nine

Jen kept walking across the soft, green grass. She came within twenty yards of the three people. They stopped moving toward her, and so she stopped. She looked at them uncertainly. Her heart was racing. She was breathing hard. Both of these things suddenly struck her. She was breathing. Her heart was pumping. These things weren't happening earlier.

As she became aware of her heart and respiration, they returned almost instantly to normal. It was different from any experience she'd ever had before. It was like... she had tried meditating once. And after hours she had been able to focus on her breathing so closely that she slowed it down. It was like that, only instantly. Her heart was beating normally and her breathing was back to a soft background sound. Then both went away entirely.

The others watched her expectantly. They were smiling slightly. On most faces, it would seem kinda creepy to see these little smiles. Or maybe daft. Or perhaps condescending. But those expressions were entirely foreign to these faces. These faces could only radiate one thing: love.

She couldn't figure out the A/S/L of the three beings. They all looked like they were about her age... early twenties. But there was something beyond ancient in their expressions. She would have no trouble believing that one of them had built the pyramids.

They didn't seem to be obviously men or obviously women. They were all three so incredibly beautiful that they defied her ability to categorize them. They all had long hair, two of them dark brown, one light brown, almost blond. They wore white terrycloth robes like the one she was wearing.

She was certain that they were... other. They were not "from here", you might say. But beyond that she was at a loss. Were they aliens? Gods? Angels? Dead people in the afterlife? She wasn't sure what she believed about any of those things. But she was face to face with them now, so it was clear that they were something in heaven and earth more than she'd dreamt of in her philosophy. As the bard might say, from her English class in high school.

As she stood before them, she felt things change. The light shifted. It didn't grow brighter so much as it... seemed to infuse everything. There was a glow. She felt something relax inside of her. Her whole body followed suit. Muscles she didn't realize she had suddenly soothed and her body shifted its position as she became more comfortable than she'd ever been. Her body all of the sudden FIT her in a way it never had before. Like a glove had somehow become part of her hand.

She felt... a peace so powerful it almost knocked her down. She was swept away on the waves of it for what seemed like hours. Tears coursed down her cheeks as this peace swept over her in wave after wave, washing away the stress and pain of her entire lifetime. If she had been in her mortal body, she would have collapsed. But her body seemed capable of standing by itself. And so it did.

After the peace came a tsunami of searing and all-encompassing love. It was like falling into the sun, but without being burned up. She remembered something about a bush talking to... who was it? Noah? And not being consumed. She knew how that felt now. She was aflame... but she was not consumed.

The love just kept coming. The three beings looked at her, and their expressions were unfathomable. They seemed at the same time to know everything about her, but to be curious about her and to wonder about her. It was like they were studying her, while having studied her for eons. It was like they couldn't get enough of her. Which was ridiculous... they were clearly on a plane light years beyond her. She was just Jen. They were... something much more.

In their presence she knew that everything was going to be OK. Everything. They were utterly capable of making the whole universe... all universes... alright. Righting all wrongs. Wiping away every tear. Saving everyone that needed it. Fixing all that was broken. Mending the things that she couldn't even understand were needing it. All would be well, and everything would be perfect.

There was no doubt, no fear, no pain.

After she'd stood and soaked in this love for … for how long she had no way of knowing... she noticed a black dot on the horizon growing larger.

She was utterly at peace and full of love and had no worry or concern about the black dot. She watched it grow. It grew from a tiny speck to a dot to a moving thing. As she focused her attention on it, it came into focus. It was a wolf.

There was a tiny black wolf running toward her. As she watched, she saw that it wasn't tiny, it just seemed so because of distance. Compared to the trees it was passing, it was actually rather large. Bigger than she was, it seemed like.

It was running incredibly fast. Within just a few seconds, it came from the horizon to within a few hundred yards. Still she felt no fear or apprehension. She watched as it approached. She looked into its face, and recognized the eyes. They were the eyes of the young man from the hot tub.

When the wolf got about fifty yards from her, and was only about two seconds from reaching her, the three beings looked at it very suddenly. Instantly the wolf collapsed and went nose first into the grass. It lay there unmoving, except for its eyes. Jen looked at it more closely, and noticed the fur was turned up on one of its shoulders. No, on second glance it wasn't fur. It was a cricket. The cricket was also frozen in place, except for its eyes, which were moving around frantically.

Chapter Forty

Amy followed the trail. Amon followed Amy. He couldn't begin to see what she was tracing as she ran. Even if he'd crawled on his hands and knees, he couldn't have found the trail she chased after effortlessly. To say that he was impressed with her tracking skills was a magnificent understatement.

She followed the trail to a warehouse. She stopped suddenly and Amon almost ran into her. He skidded almost to a stop after swerving around her crazily. He slammed into the side of the warehouse before he could arrest his velocity. He looked at Amy sheepishly.

"Good thing we're invincible, since our element of surprise is shot," said Amy quietly.

Amon started to smile, but Amy then said, "We need to be careful. The young woman we're here to help is not so impervious to her enemies."

They moved silently around the building, and Amon watched Amy leap into an open window three stories up. He glanced around, judged the distance, and leaped. Amy caught him and set him down on the window ledge carefully. She put a finger to her lips.

'Stay here. And don't try to message me back.'

Then she was gone.

Chapter Forty-one

David sat in the lotus position and thought. He was waiting for Alisha to return. It seemed like it had been awhile since she left, but time was so very relative to him now that he wasn't sure. He knew that he sensed time as being longer when he was away from Alisha than when anything else was happening, but he was self-aware enough to realize that was because his feelings for her made time away from her seem longer.

Einstein was aware of the relativity of time in a boring lecture versus time with a pretty girl. And David had experienced both to an extreme degree. The time he spent Sphered seemed longer than his entire lifetime and the lives of all his friends put together. It was truly a torture to be separated from all stimuli for that long. He probably would not have survived it, at least with his sanity intact, if it were not for the visits from the Others.

They hadn't been with him the whole time, but they had visited with a regularity that he now missed. They hadn't said much during their visits, but they didn't need to. Just being in the presence of the Others put him at peace, gave him food for his soul (as David saw it), and filled him with a hope and love that got him through until the next visit.

On their last visit, they gave him the promise that he would be rescued soon. He knew from experience that when the Others say "soon", they mean it with the slant of Aslan – who calls all times "soon." But they were giving him hope, and intentionally so, and so he knew that they meant sooner rather than later. And just a few days later, his rescuers arrived. Not only did he see people again, he saw her.

Just as he thought this, Alisha entered the room.

'I see you,' he shot to her.

She smiled. From anyone else, this would be odd. So obvious a statement as to almost be creepy. But Alisha knew what he meant.

And what he meant. And what he MEANT.

'I see you, too,' she shot back, looking at the floor and blushing a little.

It amazed them both that they still had this sort of almost sophomoric silliness in their relationship. One might think, after all they had been through together, and after the millennia they had spent getting to relationship levels that were deeper than they had heard about or read about from anyone else, that this silly shyness would have gone away. That the thunk of the familiar would have shoved this blushing schoolgirl feeling out of the window of their relationship eons ago.

They weren't sure why it hadn't. They didn't know why their relationship still seemed fresh and new, scary and interesting and gift-like even now. But they were both grateful that it was this way. And they both hoped it always would be.

She sat down next to him and their knees touched. They sat like that for some time, just staring straight ahead, not even looking at each other, but drinking in each other's presence like they were dying of thirst.

After sitting like this for hours? Days? David finally shot to her 'Did you hear from Dorian?'

Chapter Forty-two

Jen looked at the three people. One of them looked at her in a pointed way, and this thought formed in her mind. 'You should go now. We will find you. You are safe from this one,' the person looked at the wolf, 'for now. Go into the fountain and find your way. Our power will go with you for a time.'

She wasn't sure what that meant. She turned and looked behind her, and saw, what seemed miles away, a white fountain.

She started running.

Chapter Forty-three

Alisha looked at John and frowned. He looked back at her and shrugged. 'What? You want me to go be totally invisible?'

She looked unhappy. No good answer here. She looked at David.

'What's wrong?' asked David without opening his eyes.

Alisha looked back at John and appeared so miserable that John laughed. 'OK, OK… but only cuz you're so adorable when you're miserable.'

'Is that what Hugo said?' she quipped.

'I'll be back in an hour, Cosette,' he shot back. 'And I won't be listening.'

David opened his eyes and looked at her.

'It's John,' she said.

'Oh,' he said, his face going blank.

'He just volunteered to leave… to give us some space,' she said.

'Is he in the room now?' asked David.

'He's almost out the door.'

"Thank you, John," said David out loud. His voice sounded hoarse.

'He says "yeah, yeah",' Alisha shot to David.

David laughed softly. 'Yeah, that's John alright. Is he doing OK these days? Holy shiva… I never thought about… what did he do while you were Sphered?'

'He stood outside my Sphere and talked to me,' she said softly.

David looked at her. 'Every day?'

'Every hour of every day, for three years.'

'How did … did you guys … '

'We love each other. It's not like me and you. But it's not like brother and sister. I don't know. He'll always have a very grateful part of my heart.'

David processed that.

'Should that bother me?'

'A little.'

Chapter Forty-four

When Jen was almost to the fountain, which she got to much faster than she was expecting, she looked back. The three people were gone, and the wolf was on its feet. It spotted her and took off like a shot.

She looked ahead again and almost ran into the fountain. She dove over the side and into the … she thought of it as water, but when she entered it, she didn't feel wet. She felt like she was floating in air.

She swam down into the air and looked around. She heard a sound behind her and saw the blond young man dive into the …fluid behind her. He saw her and started swimming her direction.

She cried out and it sounded strange… strangled. Like she was on something moving very fast… a motorcycle or in the back of a truck… and the wind was whipping around her, carrying her sounds away.

She didn't see the cricket, but she knew it was close. She swam madly away from him, and her adrenaline must have given her speed because she started losing him.

She heard him make an annoyed sound and could sense that he was struggling to catch her. She swam madly and blindly ahead and saw the … water-air swirling around in a strange way to her right. In desperation she swam towards that weird swirl and was sucked into it.…

She suddenly found herself standing in sand, with hot, dry sand as far as she could see all around.

She felt breath on her neck, and winced and spun around.

Immediately behind her stood a camel.

Chapter Forty-five

Bronty sat in his Sphere. He wasn't sure how long he could put up with this. He'd been in the Sphere for three days, and it was beginning to get to him. Oko couldn't expect him to last much longer in here. All he had to do was… no! He couldn't start thinking about that. If he… he knew that… once he started down that road, there would be no turning back.

He shifted his position. Tried to get comfortable for the hundredth time. He thought about his last vacation. It only made him miserable. He … needed… out…. He thought about his life before he became Ui… it seemed like so long ago, and so dreary and monochrome and lame… He yelled "Let me out of heeeeeere!" for the fiftieth time. Fifty? Maybe fifty-one. How many states were there now? When was now? If it was 1945 then there were 48 states… right? When was Alaska added? As long as I keep chasing these little rabbits I'll be ok. Keep following the white rabbits down the hole and I'll be fine. Just don't think about… don't let yourself think about the fact that you're thinking about this… cuz if you lose your connection you start thinking about how small this space is and how much YOU NEED OUT RIGHT NOW!!! He flipped around inside the Sphere. He couldn't even hurt himself to give himself something to focus on. As soon as he bruised himself he healed.

He was beginning to lose his mind. He needed out. He wouldn't last much longer.

Chapter Forty-six

Jen was lost. She had no idea where she was. She also had no idea WHEN she was, but she didn't know that. She didn't know what had happened to her, or what the fountain did. She knew that she remembered dying… and then woke up better than ever. She thought maybe this was the afterlife… but if so, then no one on earth seemed to have a clue what the afterlife was like. Because she had never heard of anything like this.

She started walking across the sand. Then she realized that she didn't need to walk because of the camel. So she went back and wrestled with the camel for a while. She finally managed to get on its back. And then after what seemed another couple hours, she managed to get it to walk sort of in the direction she wanted to go. Of course, she had no idea which direction to go. But she figured if she was in a hot place and she went north, she would probably find a cooler place. That's about all she had to go on. So she figured out from the movement of the sun which way was north and she started nudging the camel that direction.

But then she remembered that she wasn't hot. Or sweating. Or breathing. And she remembered being able to run incredibly fast. Much faster than she could manage to get the stubborn camel to move. So she jumped off and started running. The camel followed her for a while until she lost it. She would have worried about just abandoning it, but it seemed no worse off now than before, as close to the middle of nowhere as it had been when she found it. So she kept running.

She ran for almost an hour. She couldn't tell the passage of time, only that the sun was a little farther across the sky when she saw the pyramid.

Chapter Forty-seven

Amon waited in the window on the second floor of the warehouse. He looked down into the warehouse and could see perfectly well, since his sight seemed to be able to make out anything no matter how dark it was. At first it seemed strange, but he was getting used to this new body. Well, the newness of his old body. Or, however that worked. It was the same body he had before, but it was perfect now. He could do anything.

This puzzled him, though, and he wished Amy were still here so he could ask her. He seemed all caught up and didn't feel like he had many if any questions left while he was with her. But then she would go do something like this, and he started wondering. Like... when you're Sphered, why can't you just break out? Seems like it would be easy, if you were "able to do anything" like they told him when he was first training. Maria had said it just like that. "You can do anything now." But he didn't feel like he could do anything.

Amy had said that the Sphere moved when you did. But what about when the Sphere was held still? Like when someone was holding it... or when it was in a setting? He'd seen a Sphere in a setting, like a ring setting. What then? When the Sphere was held still, why couldn't the Ui trapped inside then be able to get to the side of the Sphere and break out?

He couldn't figure out how the Spheres kept the Ui and the DaiUi inside of them. If he could do anything, couldn't he figure that out? And if he could do anything, couldn't he break out of a Sphere? But on the other hand, if he could do anything, couldn't he invent a Sphere that the Ui could NOT break out of? Which was it?

Amy would make it make sense, in her perfectly patient way. He just needed to ask her. He needed to remember these questions so he could ask when he saw her again. He realized that he never got bored anymore. He wasn't exactly sure what boredom was, so he had difficulty examining why he wasn't bored now. It probably had something to do with the brain growing accustomed to its surroundings and then becoming, in a sense, tired of them. Same with people. They say that familiarity breeds contempt. So you would think that the Ui would all hate each other tremendously.

But the opposite was true. The more the Ui spent time together, the more they seemed to care about each other. They never seemed to grow tired of their surroundings. They never seemed to grow tired of anything.

Amon wondered if entropy had anything to do with it. Had they stopped experiencing entropy? They weren't aging. If they were wounded, which was very difficult to do, they healed almost instantly. So what relationship did entropy have with them? And, come to think of it, what relationship did entropy have with being bored? Amy had mentioned this on the sub, but it was one of the many things she said they would get back to later.

Being bored seemed, upon reflection, to be the opposite of being interested. Yes, he couldn't imagine being both bored and interested at the same time. So it would seem that the Ui were interested all of the time. And that seemed to bear up under scrutiny. He couldn't remember not being interested in things ever since he came out of that fountain. Everything was suddenly fascinating.

But then he wondered what the relationship was between entropy, physical weariness, and being bored. Clearly entropy caused normal mortal humans to feel tired. So did being physically tired contribute to being bored? He thought he could remember times when he had plenty of energy, just didn't "feel like" doing anything. And that meant boredom. And he remembered times when he was really physically tired, but still interested in what he was doing. So no, they didn't seem to be corollaries.

He never thought to himself "what is taking Amy so long?" or "where IS she??" He just sat in the window, never growing tired of sitting, never getting uncomfortable, and wondered how things worked.

Amy suddenly popped up into the window next to him. He hadn't even seen her coming. She was fast and quiet. She said, "You ok?"

"Yeah, just waiting for you. Did you find out where the blood came from?"

"Yes. She's down here. I need your help."

And just like that, all of his questions vanished.

Chapter Forty-eight

Alisha sighed.

'What's wrong?' asked David.

'I sent John away ... rather, he volunteered to go away... so that I would have some time with you. And as soon as he's gone, he came between us. Now we feel all awkward.'

'Yeah... ironic, isn't it.'

Alisha pressed her lips together and blew out of her nose. 'We never get a break, do we?'

'Well there was that one time.' David said, glancing at her impishly.

She blushed. 'I thought we were never going to mention that again.'

'Oops.'

He took her hand.

She never felt as close to anyone in her life as she did right then.

And she was overwhelmed with happiness that she didn't feel distracted or torn or lured away from him. In this moment, it was just Alisha and David.

If only it could stay like this. If she could push a button and freeze this moment forever, she would. But that button had never been made, or she hadn't found it yet.

She ran her finger across the back of his hand, smiled ruefully, and tried with all of her might to savor the moment. While it lasted.

She put her head on his chest. It felt like a surrender, but even when she stretched, she couldn't reach to see what she was surrendering to. But it felt right, it felt good.

She whispered, aloud, "I'm sorry."

He squeezed her hand.

She whispered "Thank you. For everything."

After what seemed like years, he shot her a picture. It was of her, looking out of a window, looking lost and sad and desperate.

'You found me,' he sent. 'You… have me.'

She looked grateful and happy and miserable and scared all at the same time. Tears filled her eyes, and one streaked down her cheek and onto his chest.

'I know' he sent her. She received another pic, of her walking out of the door with her head down. 'It might happen again. It probably will. But we're here now. And I will always be here for you.'

Tears streamed down her face.

"I don't deserve you," she whispered.

'I know,' he sent, and she choked a giggle. Then he sent, 'I don't deserve you either. Someone sent us as gifts to one another.'

She turned her face down and her body shuddered as she wept.

'I love you.' Does it matter who said it?

Chapter Forty-nine

Amon looked down at the teenage girl lying on her side in the dirt and oil. She was breathing, but just barely. Her hands and feet were tied up with plastic quick ties, and her shorts were unfastened at the top. She still had her t-shirt on, but it was torn and pulled halfway up her back.

Amy crouched down by the girl and popped the quick ties easily with one hand. She pulled the girl's shirt into a more modest position and fastened her shorts. She picked her up and carried her to the edge of the warehouse. She jumped to the window, and motioned with her chin for Amon to follow her.

When they were safely and quietly outside, she handed the girl to Amon. 'Take her to that van at the end of the road, the one we passed coming in? The red one? Don't try to answer me, just nod if you remember.'

Amon nodded.

'Good. Take her there and guard her. She's stable and should be OK until I catch up with you.'

Amon whispered so quietly that Amy barely heard him. She was proud of him for being so quiet. "What are you doing to do?"

'I'm going to find who did this.' The cold glint in her eyes scared Amon. He was glad he wasn't on the receiving end of that glare.

He ran off with the girl toward the van. Amy turned, leaped into the window, and vanished inside, her eyes flashing.

Chapter Fifty

Jen saw groups of people carrying things back and forth to the pyramid. It looked like it was almost complete, and she had never seen anything so amazing in her life. She had seen pictures of the pyramids many times, but they were ancient and yellow and eroded in the pictures she had seen. This was a brand-new pyramid, and it was astounding.

In the pictures she had seen, the pyramids were always out in the middle of a bunch of sand. But these were surrounded by vivid civilization. There were vibrant colors and fountains all around them, and bustling business going on everywhere she looked.

But nothing outshone the pyramid. It was easy to see why the people used to worship at the base of this fantastic structure. It was eye-blindingly white, whiter than she thought a building could be, and capped with a little golden pyramid on top. When the sun hit it at the wrong angle, she couldn't even look at it directly. The word dazzling seemed like it was invented to describe the thing she was looking at.

She had time to notice all of this before she was noticed herself. Then it was time for evasive action. She evaded.

Chapter Fifty-one

Amy closed her eyes, and in the next few seconds she ceased to look like Amy. She then looked exactly like the girl who she had just found on the floor. Her hands and feet were even bound with plastic quick ties, just like the girl. She sat down in the oil and dirt, and then fell over into the position she'd found the girl in. She waited.

She didn't have to wait long. She thought it might be hours, but less than five minutes later, the door opened, and seven big men, all in their twenties and thirties, and all carrying firearms, entered the warehouse. They closed the door.

They ambled over to where she was lying, joking and shoving each other. They made crude jokes about who got to go first. They bragged about the grocery store they had just robbed. They boasted about the guys they were going to beat up later that night, maybe even kill a few of them. They resolved Amy to her decision.

They formed a circle around her, and one of them reached down to smack her face. As he swung, suddenly his hand was caught in her hand, she flipped him over onto his back, and with a quick smack to the side of his head, knocked him out.

She stood up, snapping the tie that had been around her ankles. The men grinned and circled around her. After seeing her dispose of their friend so easily, they should have had some worries, maybe even tried to take off. Evidently, they weren't the brightest bunch.

She said, "If any of you want to leave, I'm going to give you one last chance." They all laughed. It was an ugly sound.

They weren't worth her trouble…she decided to finish them quickly.

Chapter Fifty-two

Amon gently set the girl down on the street, opened the van, and then lifted her in. Even though he could lift her as easily as if she weighed nothing, it was still awkward moving her around, and he bumped himself and herself into the door frame and the edge of the seat a few times before getting situated. Every time he did something like that, he realized that he still needed a lot of training.

He still wasn't used to his new abilities. He supposed that was normal. That it took a while for people to get used to being strong enough to lift anything, so fast that people couldn't see him move, able to leap tall buildings… hm. Superman. *Ubermensch*. He guessed there was a part of his Aryan brain that appreciated the irony that he had to die to become the superman that his party had always dreamed that he would be.

This was no evolution, though. No superior genetics or eu-anything program had brought him here. Yes, it was all scientifically explained. And he understood most of it. Maria had been very thorough and very patient in explaining how it all worked. He still had some questions… he just seemed to forget them all when Amy was around.

He wasn't sure why that was. She was a little girl. He realized that she was millions of years old. But that didn't change the fact that she was, in his eyes, a little girl. He knew he respected her. That he felt safe when she was around. And that he would do anything to protect her.

But his feelings were very complicated when it came to being around her. He didn't really understand his own brain. He felt both in awe of her, and protective of her. He cared for her deeply, but the thought of any kind of romantic relationship just felt… out of place. Like the idea of putting your knee on someone's nose. It just felt weird and wrong and foreign.

So why did his questions fly out of his head every time she came into the room? What did he feel for her? He wasn't sure. He knew he liked it. She meant more to him than anyone he'd known in his former life, before being changed into Ui. He was beginning to think that relationships now would be different than anything he'd experienced in his former life. Even romantic relationships were different now. It was a scary thought to consider entering into a romance with someone, when you knew you would be with them for thousands of years. That was a serious commitment.

He knew it was unusual for Ui to get married. It had happened. And it had worked. There were some couples who had remained together and in love for centuries. But there were failures, too. The most painful to learn of were the times when one person in the couple had turned and become DaiUi. It had only happened a couple times. But it was horrific to think about.

He looked down at the girl in the van. She was mercifully asleep. Or unconscious. He wasn't sure what the difference was at this point. As long as she woke up, he guessed that they were kind of the same thing at this point. The difference would be in how she got this way… knocked out or just fell asleep.

He wondered if the lack of sleep would start to make him feel strange. So far it hadn't… he'd been too busy to really notice. But eventually would it start to all run together? Did he need sleep to break up his life into manageable segments?

He wondered who he could ask about that. Right about then the girl opened her eyes, looked at him, and started to scream.

Chapter Fifty-three

Amy looked around the warehouse. Everyone was lying on the floor except for her. Most were groaning and nursing various wounds. Some were staring at her in wonder and disbelief.

She went to the leader of the group, picked him up with one hand, and slammed him against the wall. He was clearly shaken and scared, but he put on a brave face and stared her in the eye.

"If I catch you doing anything like this again, it won't go so well for you next time," she said, holding his glare. He started to mouth off, but she looked at him hard, and his mouth froze. He looked more upset about that than anything else. He didn't seem to understand why he couldn't speak. His eyes grew wide and he trembled.

"Go find something useful to do. Stop terrorizing young women. The next time you do, I will be there. And you will regret it." She looked at him hard. "Are you going to do this again?"

He nodded. Her expression grew grim, and he winced in pain. He tried to wrestle out of her grasp, but it was completely useless.

"Are you going to do this again?"

He hesitated. Then he nodded. Her eyes grew dark and he screamed. "You need to learn not to do this. As long as you keep doing it, you're hurting yourself and other people. Now think hard before you answer this time."

He looked at her and trembled.

"Are you going to do this again?"

He stared at her for several seconds. Then he shook his head.

"Good. And keep your guys from doing it too. Or I'll be back. And next time what you felt inside your brain will feel like nothing compared to what I'll do then. Go be a better person."

She tossed him onto a couple of his buddies and walked off into the darkness.

Chapter Fifty-four

'How IS John?' David asked.

Alisha looked at him gratefully. 'He's ... OK. He is still hopeful that we'll find a way to ... uninvisibilize him... so he can interact with you guys normally again. He finally got past apologizing to me. For the first few months he kept giving me the hangdog look. He always felt guilty, since he knew that he was spending time with me that you would have killed to have. But I finally convinced him that acting like that was only making both of us unhappy.'

David nodded.

'So I told him to embrace what was happening. To enjoy his time with me, and stop feeling bad about it. He saw the sense of it, and after about a week of getting over it, he started acting normally around me. Then it was great. He takes a hint really well, so when I need a little alone time, he makes himself scarce. But I know that it's got to be lonely, so I try to be as unselfish as possible and spend as much time with him as I can. But he needs some alone time every once in a while, too. So it usually works out pretty well. Of course, he doesn't need to hint to me. If he needs to be alone, he just goes away for a while.'

'Have you tried experimenting with some of the bright spots, to see if you can undo what happened?'

'Yes, we try about once a week. We have had some weird things happen, like we found a Dark Door near Auschwitz in 1946 that we didn't know was there before...'

David frowned. 'That's an odd time for it to occur.'

'We guessed maybe it was a result of the atrocities before that date, but we couldn't hit the date right on because it was too bright.'

'That does make sense.... Maybe.'

'But nothing has affected his only being visible to me at all.'

'Still haven't come up with a better way to refer to it, I see?'

'I'm not sure we really need to. You just said "I see", and I just said "You just said" when we know that neither of those things is literally true. I think it's clear enough to call John invisible when we all know it means that no one else can experience his existence at all. That he only exists to me.'

'I guess you're right.'

'How is your strength coming along?' she sent.

'Better. I think we should go for a run, actually.'

'You're still not talking, but you want to run?'

'Running is only physical, not physical and mental and emotional and social all at once, like talking is.'

'Then let's go.'

They ran up and down the halls of Sri Kaăsala.

Chapter Fifty-five

Amy climbed into the back of the van before Amon realized she was there. "How do you move so… stealthily?" he whispered.

'Lots of practice,' she sent. 'Don't try to reply.'

"I wasn't going to," he replied, a little sulkily. He wasn't sure if that was entirely true.

'What happened here?' she frowned.

"Oh," he whispered, "She started to scream, so I had to quiet her."

The girl had duct tape over her mouth, but she appeared to be sleeping.

'Is she asleep?'

"I think I … kind of knocked her out. I've never done it before, but I just thought about her being asleep, and she started looking sleepy, and then she just fell over and passed out." He looked a little worried and a little proud at the same time.

'Try it on me,' Amy said, and her eyes danced a little.

Amon looked hard at Amy. A few seconds passed.

'Wow. You're good at that. Have you tried any other kinds of coercion?'

"Is that what I'm doing? Coercing?"

'You're mentally affecting the cognitive state of another person. You're apparently a natural at it, since I don't believe Maria taught you that. Is that right?'

"She didn't teach me anything like that. She mentioned that some of these things are possible, but she never showed me how. Just like she never taught me to send messages like you're sending me."

'You'll learn that soon. It's not hard to do, it's just hard NOT to do. Once you start sending messages, you have to learn control very quickly, or you'll send all kinds of things you don't mean to. You'll tell your friends embarrassing things. You'll send messages to other people by accident. You'll tell your enemies where you are and what you're up to. You have to learn to direct your thinking very clearly to one person, and only to send what you mean to. It takes a little time, but once you've practiced it for a couple months you'll be good to go.'

Amon laughed. "I still haven't gotten used to your different sense of time. To me, if something is easy I can master it in an afternoon. You say it's easy, but it'll take me months to learn how to do it."

'You'll get used to that, too,' she sent, her eyes jumping a bit.

Chapter Fifty-six

Jen's only problem was not attracting attention to herself. It was easy to get away from the people who noticed her... she could run faster than any of them could begin to follow. But she was trying to figure out where she was. And she saw people building a pyramid... where were they building pyramids these days? The snatches of language that she overheard each time she listened, before the crowds saw her and closed in, sounded vaguely Middle Eastern... but with an odd tinge that she'd never heard before.

Jen wasn't exactly an expert in languages. She took Spanish in high school, like practically everyone else, and she didn't remember much of that. But she had heard people speaking in the Middle East on TV and in movies, and the language she heard them speaking sounded something like that.

Thinking about high school made her start to feel lost and alone. She realized she had no idea where she was, how she got there, or how to get back. She started to feel panicked and she almost cried a few times. But she pulled it together, took some deep breaths, and focused on the future.

Whatever else had happened, she seemed to have been given some weird abilities. She wasn't sure who those three people were, but they were clearly good... and good to her. They "said" they would see her again... and she found herself looking forward to that.

She didn't know where the wolf guy had gone. She hoped she never saw him or his evil little cricket again. But she had a feeling she would.

And she had a feeling it would be soon.

Chapter Fifty-seven

Amon looked at the girl. "So what are we gonna do with her now?"

Amy looked at her and sighed. 'I'm going to take the memory of her attack away. And I'm going to give her some medicine, which will heal her entirely. Basically, when I get done, none of this will have happened to her.'

"Why don't we just go back and make it so that it really doesn't happen to her?" Amon asked.

'Time travel is complicated. It's not easy to do, but it IS easy to make big mistakes. We don't just jump around at will... and it takes careful planning to make it happen. Even then, it gets botched easily.'

"If it were easy, everyone would do it?" asked Amon.

Amy shot him a look, and he wasn't sure that it wasn't an amused one. But he sensed without seeing it. She didn't smile or even dance her eyes. He just sensed that his words amused her.

'If it were to save her life, it would be worth the planning and difficulty involved. Even then we might not get it right. But since I can reverse the effects and make it, for her, like it never happened, it's a better and more responsible solution.'

"OK, then," said Amon. "Do I need to leave while you treat her?"

'No, it's very simple. You can watch.' She took a tiny vial out of her belt. She opened it and waved it under the girl's nose. She also touched the duct tape and it fell off as though it were not stuck to her. The girl seemed to relax in her sleep and breathe more calmly. Then Amy turned the vial around and put the other end to the girl's lips. Amy twisted the middle of the vial slightly, and it suddenly emptied... Amon saw the fluid shoot out and ... presumably, into the girl's mouth. The girl mumbled slightly and swallowed.

The bruises on her cheeks faded and disappeared. Her color returned to normal, and the scrapes and contusions on her arms and legs vanished. She reached, in her sleep, and scratched an itch on her belly. Then she rolled over and slept even more soundly.

"Where should we take her?"

'What do you think?'

Amon thought about it. "A hospital?"

'That works.'

Chapter Fifty-eight

Jen had to figure out where she was before she could try to go…
well, at least go back to the United States…she wasn't sure what to
do when she got there. Find her family, but then what? Go back to
work? Pretend nothing happened? Go on with her life? She didn't
know what to expect when she got back… would the wolf guy hunt
her down? That's what wolves do, right?

Well, she couldn't control all of that. She focused on what she could
change. She needed to find out where she was, and try to find a way
back home. She knew she could move really fast, so she ran as fast
as she could into the little market place between the pyramids and
grabbed some clothes and ran out again before anyone could react.
She didn't like the idea of stealing, but her options were pretty
limited at this point.

She put the clothes on, and they were a little too big, but she did
what she could with the belt and hood and after she was done it was
hard to tell her apart from the other poor women. She went back into
the market and milled around, hoping to see a map or grab a cell
phone or something to learn where she was.

After a few hours of doing this, she started to worry that she was so
far out in the middle of nowhere that she would never get home.
Everyone seemed poor here. No one had phones or even watches.
Some had really nice jewelry, but that was all she saw. And the
money that she saw people pay with, when they used money, looked
very strange. Again, she was no expert on types of currency, but she
had no idea what those little strangely shaped coins were. And she
was at a loss how to tell anyone who she was or what she needed.

It looked like she would have to steal even more. Then again, she
didn't need to eat. Or drink. Or sleep. Maybe she should just start
walking… surely she would eventually come to some kind of
civilization where they had phones and TV's and stuff?

It was worth trying. She was getting nowhere here. She walked north
until she reached the ocean. It was very beautiful. She followed the

coast east until she reached an enormous river. There were huge boats on the river, full of incredibly beautiful colors. She sat on the bank for hours, watching them.

She decided there was no reason to freak out. She had no needs. Those wonderful three people were going to find her and help her. For now, she would try to enjoy her situation. Watch people and learn, enjoy the beauty around her.

She decided this because it seemed a good idea. It also seemed to be her only option, and this kept her sane.

Chapter Fifty-nine

Amon and Amy raced back to Florida and dove into the fountain. They emerged in Sri Kaṣsala and headed to the gym.

"Now we're going to work on physics," said Amy.

She looked at Amon. "What's wrong?"

"Nothing," he said, but clearly something was.

She looked at him and raised her eyebrows very slightly.

"Nothing, it's fine," he said.

"Just go ahead and tell me," she said.

"I just got confused. I thought Maria was training me, but now it seems to be you all of the time," he said. "Don't think I mind… I'm not complaining. You're a great teacher and I enjoy learning from you… I just don't understand why I was traded off."

Amy looked at him closely. Then she said, "You weren't traded off. I asked to train you. Maria usually does the initial meditation process, and sometimes she keeps going from there. She's an excellent trainer. But if one of us feels a connection to a certain novice, we can request to be their trainer. Maria didn't feel especially close to you, and I did. I felt like we had a good bonding experience on the sub, and that it would be useful in your training."

Amon blushed. "Oh," he said. "Well, thanks."

"You said that you enjoy learning from me. I'll take you at face value. If that changes, let me know, and we can trade you off." Her eyes danced a little on the last three words.

"So you said we're going to learn physics today? Shouldn't we be in a classroom?"

"You don't learn well in a classroom. Classrooms are boring. The mind stultifies in a classroom. Old didactic systems were inherently flawed. We changed all of that, and continue to evolve our teaching systems as we learn new things. It's never experimental. We just adapt as we see new ways of teaching – or learning – are more effective."

"So we're learning physics in the gym? Where do we learn biology?"

"In nature."

"Nat-"

"Don't say it."

"What?"

"You were about to make a corny joke, and I won't stand for it."

Amon grinned and they went into the gym.

Chapter Sixty

Jen was getting a sinking feeling. She was watching the boats come up and down the huge river. She didn't understand what was happening. All of the boats looked… really old. She didn't see any modern vessels at all. Everything looked like some kind of boat exhibit. Where was she?

She started to feel panicked again. How would she ever get home if she didn't even know where she was? How would she pay for it? Who could she talk to? Maybe she should just walk up to a group of people, with women in the group, and start asking if anyone spoke English. In this day and age, someone would know English. It was the worldwide language these days.

She decided to try. She didn't see any other way to figure things out. And she was good with people… what was the worst that could happen?

She was about to find out.

Chapter Sixty-one

Amon crouched in the tiny corridor. He felt like he was in an air duct. He had watched even more movies recently with his new Ui friends. He enjoyed watching everything, from the earliest black and white silent films by the Lumiere brothers to the hyper immersive 4D sens-stravaganzas of the late 27th century, he'd seen most of the best, and a few of the worst, and much of what was in between. His new friends liked movies, and had their favorites. They sometimes visited old theaters to experience them *in situ*... but most of the time they watched them in their little theater down the hall from the discussion room, or in their private viewers.

In an improbably large proportion of movies, the hero finds himself crawling down an air duct, hiding from his enemy who usually has a machine gun. *Die Hard* with Bruce Willis was one of the best examples he remembered. He felt like that now, crouching in a long silver metal corridor, trying his best to hide from his nemesis, who moved so fast and so silently that he didn't think it was really teaching him anything about physics.

Amy would appear out of nowhere, a very serious and yet somehow exhilarated look on her face, and whack him upside the head with her enormous Q-Tip looking quarter staff. Then she would vanish again. He had only scored one quick smack against her, catching her in the back of the thigh as she streaked away. He thought he heard her squeak in alarm when he hit her, and that sound was so entertaining that it kept him smiling to himself through the next fourteen hits that she soundly scored against him in the following hours.

He was supposed to be learning physics, and he had to admit he had learned a few things. But he also thought the course was being cross-referenced with anger management, and that Amy was struggling with her grade in the subject since she was clearly taking it out on his person.

Chapter Sixty-two

Val walked in to the discussion room and saw Serena holding a Sphere.

"Isn't that.."

"Yes, it's Amy's."

"Why is it in here? Doesn't she keep it in her room?"

"Yes, but she asked me to look in on it because she's training Amon and didn't want him to be alone for too long."

"Is he ok?"

"Why don't you ask him?"

Val looked at the Sphere and then took it from her hand. He sat down and sighed. It was sometimes hard to know what to say. Somehow Amy could just rattle on, but Val hadn't learned that lesson yet. He still struggled with himself, wanting to blast the DaiUi in the Sphere with recriminations for all of the evil things he'd done to the Ui.

But that wasn't the point. David and Amy had both been strong proponents of the rehab program, and Alisha and a few others had been quick to see the wisdom behind it and back them up. Surprising everyone, Eric was an early adopter and a regular counselor in the rehab program.

But it was especially hard to talk to this one. They had Sphered one of the leader of the leaders of the DaiUi, second only to the Dark One herself. His name was Federico, and he had done worse than any of them even knew, and they knew a lot. During the first few decades of his imprisonment, he had bragged about all that he'd done, and laughed at the Ui's efforts to turn him back to the good side.

But Amy was very good at persuasion. She talked to him every day, when she wasn't out on mission. She couldn't take him on mission because he would find a way to mess things up, to put them in danger. So she left him in her room, safely in the setting on her desk, and came back when she was free to spend time with him and try to lead him back to the light.

Val took a deep breath, looked at the Sphere, and started talking to Federico.

Chapter Sixty-three

Strode surveyed the pool table. Serena had a tiny lead on him, and he intended to close that gap. He placed the cue ball in his favorite spot, lined up the shot, and broke. Every ball except the eight-ball shot into a pocket. He walked around the table, set up the eight ball in the corner, and was just about to sink it when he heard a very slight whooshing sound.

He turned around and eight motorcycles swept into the room. They made no sound as they circled the room, drew into a tight formation near the pool table, and came to a stop. Eight kids climbed off their bikes and went to the bar. They nodded to Strode and Serena and a couple of them raised their sunglasses and put them on top of their heads. The others kept them in place.

They ranged in age from looking like the youngest was about 11 to the oldest who looked around 14. All of them were much older than that, of course. But they chose to keep their look, from when they were changed.

Strode shot Serena a look, and she nodded. He sunk the eight and walked over to the cool kids.

"How'd things turn out in Miramar?" he asked casually. The cool kids didn't like pressure or awkwardness. You had to approach them very laid back, or they would just look at you.

"No problem, man," said Pedro. "We had it wrapped ages ago, but they sent another wave. But we got it cleaned up and it should stay that way for a while."

"You think so?" asked Serena.

Pedro shrugged. Serena had been a little too direct.

"Did you hear we found David?" asked Strode.

"Yeah, man," said Angela. "Very rad."

Two of the other kids looked over and nodded. They had various drinks before them on the bar, and they were lounged here and there on stools.

"Well, we're glad you made it back OK," said Serena.

Angela nodded, "Thanks, dude."

Serena had gotten used to being called "dude" by the cool kids a long time ago. She didn't put up with it from anyone else, but you didn't want to call the cool kids on it. They didn't go for that.

"I think David wants to talk to you when you get settled in," said Strode.

"Yeah, man," said Pedro. "We'll find him."

Strode nodded to them, and he and Serena headed out of the room. The cool kids drank their drinks, looked around, and chilled.

Chapter Sixty-four

Amon and Amy were sitting on the side of the pool with their legs in the water. They had been swimming laps and working on their underwater maneuvers. Amon was getting used to not having to breathe, and learning to control his movements to prepare for work in the fountain.

They sat on the side and were talking when George came into the pool area. Amy's eyes went to George, then back to study Amon's face. She seemed very intent on watching his reaction for some reason.

George came over to the side of the pool and said, "Hi, Amy. This the new guy?"

Amon stood up and stuck out his hand. "Good to meet you."

George reached out to shake his hand, but as he did so his foot slipped over the side and he tottered on the edge, his arms wind milling wildly, and he almost caught himself. Almost.

Then he lost his balance altogether and fell in. He would have hit Amy on his way in, but she dodged out of the way at the last second and he just missed her.

Amon dove in, swam over to where George was floundering, and pulled him to the side. George looked at him gratefully and said, "I'm sorry about that. I can be a little clumsy sometimes."

"No big deal. Amy and I were about to go get some dinner. Care to join us?"

"Oh… you're going to eat?" It sounded like a novel idea to George.

"Yes, I think Serena is making something Mediterranean."

"Oh, ok. Sounds like it might be worth checking out," said George.

Chapter Sixty-five

Alex and John sat under a tree in the parking lot of their high school. They passed a bottle of Coke back and forth, taking swigs and talking about nothing.

"They say you can judge the quality of a friendship by the insignificance of the things you talk about," said John.

Alex giggled. She felt closest to John when one or both of them were being silly. "Is that so?" she asked, grinning.

"Yep. The more pointless the things you share with someone, the closer you are to them. Think about it. You just told me the spot on your knee where you scraped it yesterday is feeling better. While that was interesting news to me, I doubt you would tell the President of the United States that if he came by."

"That's true. I wouldn't even tell the president of our student body that."

"Because you don't feel close to them. But with your best friend, you'll talk about anything."

Alex thought about this. "Do you think there are people out there who don't have close enough friends to talk about this kind of thing?"

"Yeah. Look at that girl." He pointed at one of the unpopular girls in the class who was sitting alone, eating a sandwich and reading a book.

"She seems nice," said Alex, a little unhappy that John was picking on her.

"Yeah, she's great. She is probably the smartest girl in our class, and I'm sure she'll have an awesome life. I've got nothing against her... but she never seems to talk to anyone. I don't think she's got someone to share stuff with like we do."

Alex liked the sound of "like we do."

She passed the bottle back to John and said, "So what are you doing this weekend?"

"Well…" John said, smiling his charming smile, "I was thinking about going on a date."

Alex's eyes widened a little and her eyebrows went up. "Really?"

"Yes. Remember I was telling you that Amanda girl in my Algebra class seemed to be flirting with me?"

Alex was stricken, but tried not to show it. "Yes."

"Well, she passed me a note today and it said she was going to a movie Saturday night with a couple friends and asked if I wanted to go."

"Oh."

"But I won't go if you're bored Saturday! You know your friendship means more to me than going out with some girl," John added quickly.

"No, you should go. I know you've been thinking about her a lot this year."

"What are you gonna do Saturday night?"

"My parents want me to go to the lake house with them."

"Oh, good. So you won't be alone anyway."

"No. You should definitely go and have fun. What movie are you going to see?"

"I don't even know what's out. I've been so buried in homework-"

Alex laughed. "I know, right? Economics…"

"… is kicking our butts," finished John. "Well, cool. I was worried about bringing it up, but I'm glad you're cool with it."

"Totally," said Alex. And she almost meant it.

Chapter Sixty-six

Amy passed the plate of tortillas to George very carefully. He still dropped it.

"I'm sorry," he said automatically, picking up the plate and using tongs to put the tortillas back on it. He missed with one and it fell into one of the many bowls of hummus. This particular bowl was made with an assortment of olives, and was Strode's favorite.

"Hey, man!" said Strode, "Careful where you're dropping stuff."

"Sorry... sorry" said George automatically. He said that word more than any other. It would be a little sad, but he seemed to have a good attitude about it, and the rest of the Ui just took it in stride... especially Strode.

"I know you're gonna drop it, just drop it somewhere else, my man!" he said, giving one of his rare smiles. Strode was a very happy person, but you usually couldn't tell by looking at his face. He looked serious, maybe even fierce, most of the time. His resting face scared people.

"I didn't know they made tortillas over in the Mediterranean area?" asked Amon.

The group smiled at the question. "Well," said Serena, "That's a good question. See, in your time they DO make tortillas in Spain, but they don't look like this." She held up a tortilla, which was a big flat circular bread-like wrap material made of corn meal and popular in Mexico and the southern United States. "In your time, in Spain, 'tortillas' are more like soufflés or omelets. However, foods and languages learn from one another. And over time, words and meals migrate from one part of the world to another. By 2150 or so," she glanced a question mark at Amy, who nodded, "this kind of tortilla is very popular all around the Mediterranean. The idea is present in so many forms in your time already, like in pita bread or nan. But the Mexican tortilla takes the Mediterranean by storm and most cultures use it in either its wheat or corn variety by the end of the 22nd century."

Amon thought about that. Then he clearly went another direction.

"So is… is John here?" he asked.

"Yeah, he's sitting at the bar," said Alisha without pausing in eating. She was so used to giving updates on John that she didn't even think about them anymore. They just popped out whenever someone asked.

"Does he say things to the rest of us very often?" asked Amon.

"Not often. He doesn't want me to feel like I'm always being his mouth. So he only shares things that we really NEED to hear, or he'll share a particularly clever *bon mot*."

"Clever phrase," translated Serena.

"I know *bon mot*," said Amon, smiling, "Does he ever eat?"

"He doesn't need to, just like none of us need to. But he eats with me sometimes. He doesn't like to eat with other people because it's happening in another dimensional plane and it's disconcerting when things overlap. So he kinda keeps to himself most of the time, just talking to me about what's going on."

"And you said this was because of a time traveling accident?" asked Amon.

There were a few smiles at the amusing expression. They had all heard the story thousands of times, but the phrase "time traveling accident" just never got old.

"Yes, it was the first time we ever used the Stream. We got too close to one of the bright spots and apparently it shifted John into another dimensional plane."

"So why can you still see him?"

"We're not sure. The only way to be sure would be to do it again, and that's probably not a good idea."

"Couldn't you do it with... like an animal or something inanimate?"

"We've played around with that a little, but getting too close to the bright spots has unpredictable results. We've lost several people into them and have never heard from them again."

"What happens to them?"

"We don't know. They vanish into the bright spot and we never get anything back from them, not even a mental message. It's like they don't exist."

"Could you send a probe?"

"We did. Several. Same thing. They vanish into the bright spot, and we never get anything back from them again. No signal. It's like they don't exist."

"So what you're saying is..."

Amy blurted, "It's like they don't exist!"

Everyone laughed except Amy. She looked down at her plate and her eyes flashed a little. This indicated a higher level of amusement than the dancing.

"So if John is on another plane, how is it that you can still see him?"

"We aren't sure if he only halfway got shifted, or if I got shifted part of the way. One way or another, I must be sharing the same plane he is somehow."

"Doesn't it make more sense that you got half-shifted since only you can see him?"

"Yes, that's the working hypothesis. But we're just not sure without having anything to compare it to."

Serena added, "We don't fully understand how the time streams work anyway. We have a general handle on the rules of using them, and can go where and when we want usually without incident. But the technology they use is beyond anything we've discovered."

"Even in the future?" asked Amon.

"Yes. As far forward as we've traveled, we still haven't encountered anyone who understood how they work."

"How did they come into existence?"

"Well, they work in conjunction with what many scientists call worm holes," Serena explained. "We don't call them worm holes, we call them the Stream. And the fountains are portals into the Stream."

"Aren't there many worm holes all over the universe?" asked Amon. He wasn't sure where he'd gotten that idea, he must have read it or seen it in a movie.

"Those are also portals into the one stream," explained Serena.

"As far as we know," clarified Amy.

Serena got up and moved some things around on the stove in the adjoining kitchenette. She seemed to be sautéing something. It smelled amazing.

"Well, yes, it's possible that there are other 'worm holes' that we haven't discovered. But every 'worm hole' we've found is just another portal into the same Stream," Serena said.

"So you just jump into the Stream and swim to whatever place you want and then get out?"

"Well, I wouldn't use the word 'just', making it sound easy or simple. It's neither. It's tricky, and it's easy to get lost or make terrible mistakes and end up who knows where or when? But yes, the general idea is that you get into the Stream, travel to where and when you choose, and then get out. One little slip and you can end up somewhere or somewhen you're not sure about, and then it's a great deal of work getting back."

"Do you have you get out where there is a fountain?"

"No. But it's preferable. Because it gives you your bearings… and it allows you to reenter the Stream if you need to. But you can get out anywhere or anywhen. You'll be trained to ascertain your ambient time and location."

"We started working on that a few hours ago," said Amy.

"It went great," said Amon ruefully.

Chapter Sixty-seven

Oko sat on his mat. He was deep in meditation. He did not tolerate disturbances lightly when he was meditating. He had kept Bronty's Sphere in his meditation chamber with him for several days. But he got annoyed with the constant, and very banal, stream of despairing nonsense that Bronty seemed to be a perpetual fount of. So he moved the Sphere into the same chamber where they had kept Alisha. He had one of his minions keep an eye on the Sphere to let him know if anything changed.

That minion came into Oko's meditation chamber and waited. He knew the consequence of interrupting, even with news of this magnitude.

Oko sensed that the news was important, so he only made the minion wait an hour. Then he opened his eyes and gestured for the little man to speak.

"Bronty's Sphere…" he started.

"Bring it to me."

The little man bowed, scurried out, and returned a few seconds later holding a Sphere.

It was red.

Chapter Sixty-eight

Amon and Amy were swimming laps. As they did so, he was practicing sending mental messages. Swimming helped him relax and concentrate. He got too antsy if he just sat and tried to do it. He could swim without even thinking about it, and so as he did his laps he composed and shot Amy one message at a time.

Amy sent, 'You're doing well. Most people have embarrassed themselves dozens of times by now. You've only done it twice.'

Amon knew she was teasing him, but he refused to take the bait. He was taking this seriously, because he wanted to go on mission sooner rather than later. He felt useless sitting around "training" when there was a world to save out there.

'Yes, but it'll still be there when you get done,' shot Amy, responding to his thought when he hadn't meant to send it. Cuss word, he thought.

'So Spheres are always white?' he sent, keeping it terse so he had more control and didn't ramble. He tended to oversend when he rambled.

'As long as the person inside of them is still there, they stay white.'

'I thought people couldn't escape from a Sphere?'

'There is only one way to escape from a Sphere.'

Amon didn't bother to ask. He could tell from her tone that she would make him figure it out. Amy was always didactic, even in her silences.

He thought. What would be the one way to escape? To enter another dimension? Is there a way that the Ui could move from one dimension to another and escape the Sphere by being in a universe that didn't have it?

'Getting colder,' Amy sent him.

Cuss. She wasn't supposed to hear that.

'You should cut down on your cussing. It makes you sound stupid,' she teased.

Apparently he was embarrassing himself regularly now. Amy. Hey Amy. Can you hear me now? Hmmmm... nothing. Maybe he had it back under control. Or maybe she was just ignoring him. How could he know? If you can hear me, say something. OK, good.

'I can't hear you now. But I'll clarify what I said. In a way you're right. But not in the way that you were thinking.'

So we DO move to another dimension, in a way of speaking. What does that mean? Surely it didn't... no.

'By self-terminating?'

'Yes. The only way to escape a Sphere besides someone unSphering you is to self-terminate.'

'How do we do that again? We just ... choose to?'

'Yes. Good send, by the way. You're getting better at this. I didn't hear anything in the interim between "just" and "choose" just now.'

Amon smiled as he swam.

'You have to decide to self-terminate. And then you say the Oath of Desolation. The reason that this was created was so that no one would ever self-terminate on accident. You repeat the Oath of Desolation seven times. And the seventh time, you no longer exist. You "die", as we used to think of it when we were mortals.'

'And then what?'

'And then nothing. And then you're dead.'

'You don't believe in … heaven or hell or whatever? Nirvana? Anything?'

'Oh, we all believe things. But none of us know. I'm only telling you what we know.'

'Do the Others tell us anything about what happens next?'

'Yes.'

'What do they say?'

'They say you have to ask them yourself.'

'They…. What, they say that every time?'

'Yes. Any time you ask them what happens after this life, they talk to you about it. But they tell you very sternly that if anyone asks about it, they need to talk to them personally about it. Not to share what they tell us individually.'

'Why not?'

'It's very personal.'

Amon mulled that over as he swam.

'So if someone self-terminates… the Sphere doesn't stay white?'

'Right.'

'What color does it turn?'

Chapter Sixty-nine

Jen wasn't sure what hell was like, or even if she believed in it. But she didn't think it could be much worse than this.

She was in a nasty little prison cell in some forsaken little corner of some backwards town in the middle of nowhere. No one spoke her language. No one listened to her or tried to help. They all acted like she had done something very wrong. And she couldn't figure out what it was.

She had tried to talk to a few of the people in the marketplace, and at first it seemed to work. They took her to more and more important looking people, though all of them very middle eastern poor third world country looking.

They talked a weird kind of gibberish to her, and she couldn't understand a single word. She tried speaking English to them, and was surprised that absolutely no one spoke it. She thought that people spoke English in every country these days. She was right, but she didn't realize which days she was in.

Things started taking a bad turn when she was taken to someone who appeared to be some kind of royalty. He asked her questions, and she of course didn't understand them. He drew pictures in some sand on a pedestal beside him. She looked at them, and they looked a lot like hieroglyphs. But she didn't know what he was asking or what he wanted.

Then they beat her and threw her into this prison. The beating hurt, even though it didn't produce any lasting bruises or wounds. They kept a close guard on her and seemed to think she was dangerous. She couldn't figure out why in the world she would be dangerous.

They brought some old, weird looking men to see her. The men waved their staffs around her and burned some powders and said some words over and over. She just looked at them and frowned. They seemed to be doing some kind of weird magic. It would have been funny if she hadn't been so scared.

After what seemed like hours passed, she fell into a state of rest, like sleep but not. She dreamed that those three people from the grassy place were in her cell with her. They went to the door of the cell and pushed it open. They looked at the guards and the guards fell asleep immediately. They took Jen by the hand and led her out of the prison and to the river. Then they went down the river for miles with her. They never said anything, but their peaceful smiles gave Jen peace and made her feel that everything would be OK.

After traveling for miles down the river, they came to a strange cave in the side of a small hill. They took a small black rock with a tiny white line around one end and placed it in an alcove in the cave. A door opened, and they entered a corridor in the back of the cave. They came to a fountain, and they indicated that Jen should enter it.

Jen came fully awake. She felt worse than she had, maybe ever in her life. She had had so much hope and peace in the dream. Waking up, and realizing that she really was in this prison cell, was like the reverse of waking up from a nightmare.

She determined that she would leave the prison that day. Or die trying.

Chapter Seventy

Buru, Kuri, and Kuru sat on meditation mats, folded into lotuses. The other Atachis were floating in the pool. All had their eyes closed and looks of concentration on their faces.

They had been assigned. Their mission was important, and they knew it would take all of their skill and cooperation as a single-minded team to keep it together.

They were going on mission with… George.

George was … they avoided the word "allowed" because the Ui were not prohibited from anything. They weren't in the military or a religious order… they didn't "work" for the Ui. It was more helpful to think of them as a family. George wanted to go on the next mission. And David, after much consultation with Alisha, Strode, and Eric, said OK.

Then he immediately called the Atachis and asked their help. They smiled and agreed.

They weren't smiling now. They were focused. They had to make sure that George not only didn't endanger anyone on the mission, but that he couldn't tell that he was being … helped along the way. It was important to everyone that George not feel like he was causing the team any hardship.

Everyone cared about George. They loved him like … well, like the brother that he was.

And they knew that he could cause the entire mission to fail, by dropping something important, or sending his thought message to the wrong person, or breaking out of cover at the wrong moment. The Ui had even, in the past, created "missions" for George to go on that did not require facing any real enemies or doing anything that might cause danger for the Ui's members.

But George heard about the new mission coming up. There was someone in need… they had heard from Monitoring that someone had been Changed without their knowledge. Someone was one of them now… but didn't realize they had the gift. And they were in danger. They needed to be rescued and then trained. And when George heard about it, he immediately volunteered.

They couldn't demure. He had been trained. And trained. And trained. He just had a hard time getting it. He seemed to get proficient at one thing, but lost his abilities in other areas. The other members kept working with him, and no one even thought about giving up. But when it was time for a mission, and George got it in his head he was going to go…

Well, he would need some help. And the Atachis were just the ones to give it. So they prepared themselves. They focused their minds and they shared plans, strategies, insights. They talked about possible dangers and tried to see eventualities.

It would take all of their skill and some luck, but they might pull it off.

Chapter Seventy-one

Alex waited under the tree for John to arrive. They never said anything about this meeting time... they just did it every day. Except... it was starting to seem... for today.

She knew that John was supposed to go on his date tonight. But she was hoping to talk to him this afternoon before he went home to get ready. He had never not shown up before. She hated that she felt this way, but there was a tiny place inside of her, for some reason right around her stomach, that felt panicked. That felt hollow. That made her wanna throw up.

She started to make excuses as her defense mechanisms kicked in. He probably had a lot to do and needed to get a head start. He probably left her a note in her locker and she missed it. He probably...

She felt arms reach around from behind her and pull her into a hug. You would think she'd be worried it was some creeper, but she could tell from 1,000 things that it was John. The smell. The sleeves. The scar on his right hand. OK, maybe it was three things, but it felt like 1,000...She felt her entire body flood with warmth and relief. She tried not to, but her eyes misted up a little.

John spun her around, kissed her forehead, and said, "I've gotta hurry. I've got so much to do. I left a note on your locker... did you get it?"

She laughed and shook her head and wiped away the little tears.

Chapter Seventy-two

Strode walked down the hallway with the ancient little old African American woman. "Are you hungry today, Annie?"

She shook her head. "Course not. We never get hungry, remember?"

Strode smiled. For some reason, her cantankerousness was endearing to him. Not all of the Ui felt this way. Amy, for some reason, had a hard time talking to Annie. Strode never had any trouble.

"Did I ever tell you that you remind me of someone?" he asked.

"Yes, you tell me that every time you see me. I haven't lost my memory, you know," she said, shaking her finger at him.

"What was my favorite thing about that particular person?" asked Strode.

"You don't have to quiz me every time you see me," she said irritably.

"I bet you forgot," teased Strode.

A tiny smile tugged at the corner of Annie's wizened old mouth, but she fought it. She loved Strode more than she could say, and she showed it the way many aged people do – by bickering and prodding and interacting in an irritable fashion that drove many young people crazy.

"Would you like to go swimming today?" he asked.

"I guess that wouldn't be so bad," she acquiesced.

They headed down the hall toward the pool room. She put her hand in the crook of his elbow.

Chapter Seventy-three

Alisha was in the rec room with the cool kids. Amon was at the bar, asking for recommendations of what to drink. The cool kids never got tired of recommending things. They seemed to accept Amon pretty quickly, with little hesitation. This was unusual. It could take years before they warmed to a new person. They still, after centuries, had difficulty being in the same room with Eric. They cared about him, they'd saved his skin dozens of times and he'd returned the favor, but they just had trouble being around him. He was loud and brash and rough. They always found other things to do whenever he was around. He understood, though it made him a little sad. He liked the cool kids. Everyone did.

'What is this drink called?' Amon asked in a group send.

'This is a Fuzzy Cucumber,' sent Rey. Rey was the quietest of all the cool kids. For her to be talking to Amon after only knowing him for a few days was amazing. Alisha didn't watch directly, but she was very aware of the conversation from where she sat checking her messages.

'What's in it?' he asked, looking at it curiously. The kids had a row of 17 drinks lined up at the bar for him to try. They were still making more. Most were in the cooler rack that ran the length of the bar and kept drinks nice and cold until they were imbibed.

'Fuzzy's Vodka, Sprite, cucumber juice... and a secret ingredient you have to guess,' Pedro volunteered. A couple of the kids suppressed chuckles.

Amon sipped it appreciatively, and glanced at their motorcycles parked around the room.

'How do those things run so quietly?' he asked, licking his lips and frowning as he tried to place the "secret ingredient".

'They're electric. Battery powered,' sent Angela, playing with her long black hair.

'How do you charge them? Is the secret ingredient a kind of food??' he asked, trying to place the taste.

'We don't charge the bikes. They're powered off of our batteries. Our boots,' sent Rey. She held one of her black boots up for him to examine.

'You'll get yours before you go on mission,' sent Pedro.

Amon looked at the cool kids' feet. He noticed, for the first time, that although they all had different styles, everyone had on black boots. Pedro's looked like cowboy boots. Rey's looked like Uggs. But they were all very dark black, and had the same flat black color.

'The batteries are in your boots?' he sent. 'Is it… gunpowder??'

The cool kids all looked at each other and smiled. 'Good job! It takes most people longer to place it,' sent Veronica.

'And no, they're not IN the boots. They ARE the boots,' said Rey, holding her Ugg up for him to admire.

'How do you charge them? How long do they last?' he asked. He seemed a never-ending font of curiosity. Maybe that was what endeared everyone to him so quickly.

'Every time we come in contact with an energy source, they absorb energy. Like right now, they're absorbing light energy from the room. They're absorbing sound energy. They're absorbing kinetic energy. If we turned up their absorption rate, it would be totally dark, silent, and very cold in here because they would be absorbing too much of the heat, light, sound, et cetera from the room,' explained Veronica.

'When we go places where there is tons of energy, like when we come near a star, their absorption rate automatically increases,' sent Pedro.

'What happens when they get topped off?' inquired Amon.

'It never happens. The battery boots can hold more energy than we'll ever put in them,' explained Rey.

'How long do they hold all this energy?' Amon asked, sipping his Fuzzy Cucumber.

'The rate of decay is very small. They'll still have 99 percent of the initial energy amount after thousands of years. They're almost perfect batteries. They hold an enormous amount of energy for a very long time and you can turn the rate of absorption or dispersal up or down from a tiny trickle to a powerful flood,' said Rey.

'How far in the future did these come from?' asked Amon, clearly impressed.

'Only a couple hundred years,' said Veronica, like it was nothing.

'Whoever invented these things…' postulated Amon.

'Was rewarded with beheading immediately,' finished Rey sadly.

'Now that's a story I've got to hear,' said Amon, looking shocked.

Alisha gasped. Everyone turned and looked at her.

"I've gotta go," she said out loud. "I just got a message. I've gotta leave right now."

She looked at Amon. "Tell David I'm sorry."

And she vanished.

Chapter Seventy-four

Alex sat on her bed. She played with her phone. She flipped through pages on her computer, flipped through pages of her school textbook, flipped through pages of a teen magazine. She was trying to keep her mind off of John and his date, trying to think of something else. Anything else. THERE WAS NOTHING ELSE.....

She decided to go for a run. That usually took her mind off of everything. She changed into her running shorts and sports bra, put on her brand-new tennis shoes, and grabbed a towel. She headed out of her room and hit the playlist on her phone for working out. A dance remix of a Katy Perry song started to play through her earbuds and she was headed out of the front door of her house when her phone pinged, letting her know she got a text.

She glanced at the screen. It was from John. It said, "imy".

She stopped her music, went back to her room, and sat on the bed. Her mind swirled. Why would he say that when he was headed on a date? Was he TRYING to drive her crazy??

She tapped into her phone, "lol aren't you supposed to be thinking about your date?" and hit send.

A few seconds later "lol i am. but i miss my bf"

Stupid boy. Why couldn't he just make it clear. Why couldn't she just find another boy to like, one who obviously liked her back. So many boys flirted with her at school... made it clear they wanted to go out. Why was she hooked on the one that obviously friend zoned her months ago??

But had he? That's what was agonizing. "Why would he be texting me if he's in love with her?" she whispered to herself.

She typed "imyt" and hit send.

What else could she do?

Chapter Seventy-five

David called a meeting and everyone was there. Everyone except Alisha.

"OK so what do we know?" he asked hoarsely.

Amon looked unhappy. "Not much. We were all at the bar talking about batteries when she suddenly got a message."

"From whom?" David demanded.

"I'm sorry. I don't know. She said she had to go. She sounded shocked… unhappy. Something was wrong, obviously. She said to tell you she was sorry, and then she just disappeared."

"Did she go through the fountain room?" he asked the Atachis.

Buru nodded. "Yes, she 'ported to the fountain room and dove in a few seconds later. CCTV picked it up."

"Any trace where she went?"

"Her tracker says she went into the fountain, headed into the Stream, and then took the second dark door on the left," reported Kuri. The Atachis were good at tracking and surveillance. And all of the Ui wore trackers in case something like this happened.

"And I'm assuming nothing after that?" David looked around morosely.

Everyone shook their heads. Amy said quietly, "I've asked my captive. He doesn't have any information on her whereabouts. I'm pretty sure he's not lying."

"Thank you," David muttered. "Did she seem under duress?"

Amon thought about it. The cool kids thought about it.

They all shrugged. "Couldn't tell. I'm sorry," said Amon. "She was obviously upset, but it wasn't clear if she was being ordered to leave or was worried about someone else."

"Well, I guess we wait, then," David said, stating the obvious.

"Pretty helpless feeling," mumbled Eric.

"We can do anything… but right now, we can do nothing," Amon seemed to be thinking out loud.

"If anyone has any more to tell me, or if you discover something, send it right away," David said, sounding almost a little desperate. It hurt to hear the pain in his voice.

Everyone wandered out. Amy took Amon back to the pool area and they did more laps. Practiced sending tight messages. Learned more about Ui technology.

And everyone waited to hear what happened to Alisha.

Chapter Seventy-six

Jen sat in her cell, trying with all of her might to figure out how to get out. She looked at the crust of nasty bread that had been shoved under the door to her cell. She glanced at the disgusting cup of tepid, rank water that had come with it. She didn't know what had happened to her when that wolf guy stabbed her in that pool, but whatever it was, it changed her.

Sometimes she felt like she was in heaven. When she met with those three people, when she was in the dream with them… she felt like everything was amazing and perfect and would go on being better and better forever.

When the wolf guy was chasing her, she still felt the peace and strength of those people traveling with her. She felt that she would succeed in escaping from the wolf and would be OK.

When she was traveling, she would get panicked a few times… she felt lost and alone. But she knew she would be OK. She knew she would figure it out.

But here in prison, she felt like she had descended into some kind of hell. All of her assurance and confidence and peace had evaporated. She felt them again during the dream, but then when she woke up the contrast was even worse than the gradual descent had been. From heaven to hell in the blink of an eye. It almost crushed her.

She went to the door of the cell and started to beat on it in frustration. To her shock, it flew off of its hinges and slammed against the opposite wall in the outside corridor.

She looked out into the corridor tentatively. There was no one there. She had no idea what time of day it was, since she couldn't see out. She crept along the corridor and heard voices. She recognized them as being those of her guards.

She looked around furtively, but didn't see anywhere to hide. She tried to disappear into the wall and be invisible… she strained to press herself into the corner and tried to be as small as possible, hoping against hope that they might somehow miss her.

Three guards came around the corner. They walked right by her without stopping. They went to her cell, saw the door lying in the corridor, and started yelling. They ran out, again running right by her without noticing her, and sounded some kind of horn alarm.

She took this opportunity to make herself scarce.

Chapter Seventy-seven

Alex ignored her phone. She worked on her homework. She watched TV. She ignored her phone. She didn't look at it. She didn't listen for the ping saying she got a message. She didn't CARE if she got one.

She took a walk, and didn't even take her phone with her. This was dangerous, since she couldn't call for help if someone tried to abduct her (not that anyone ever tried this), but she was living dangerously. She was Austin Powers.

She didn't even look at her phone when she came back from the walk, so she didn't notice that there wasn't a message for her. She took a shower and ignored her phone.

When her phone pinged at 10:07 that night, she waited 8 seconds before she grabbed it to see who it was from.

It was from John.

He was home from the date. It went OK. He didn't think she was that into him. She seemed bored the whole time, and just talked about herself, and was really boring and lame and played on her phone the whole time and he didn't think he liked her anymore.

Alex couldn't stop the smile that spread across her face.

She typed, "Chill?" and hit send.

She didn't even pretend to ignore her phone. She watched it until it pinged.

":)"

Chapter Seventy-eight

Amon swam laps. He did math equations in his head. When he got an answer, he would send it to Amy.

'Correct,' she sent back.

He did more math while he swam. He sent more answers.

'You forgot to factor the square of 973,' she sent.

He was pleased that was the reply. It meant, while he got the math slightly wrong (entirely wrong! Amy would say) he was getting the hang of sending mental messages.

If any of his computations or internal monologue came through, Amy would send him a mental image of a red flag. It was a simple negative feedback that worked perfectly.

Amy was in another part of Sri Kaăsala, working on who knows what. Maybe she was talking to her Sphere. She wasn't sharing her activities with him, just monitoring from the other room.

This was a development that also brought Amon a sense of satisfaction. He had not yet graduated to sending other people messages. But he had gotten pretty adept at sending them only to Amy.

He sent her a joke. 'What's green and has wheels?'

She sent back a face '-_-'

'Grass! I was just kidding about the wheels.'

She didn't reply.

Chapter Seventy-nine

Tim knew he shouldn't be here. He hated when Derrick talked him
into things. But here he was, ducking down this alley when he
should be at school.

"What are we doing here??" he asked once again.

"You gotta SEE this," said Derrick for the third time.

He didn't even want to see whatever it was. He wasn't even worried
about hurting Derrick's feelings, and he didn't want to impress him.
He wasn't sure why he came with him when Derrick asked him to
take off from recess and cut through the hole in the fence.

"The teachers are gonna freak OUT when we're not back from
recess! I can't fail fifth grade!" said Tim again.

"By the time they realize we're not back, we'll BE BACK!" said
Derrick again.

They had both lost count of how many times they'd had these
conversations.

"What are we DOING HERE???"

"Look!" said Derrick finally.

Tim looked. At the end of the alley was a window, and through the
window you could see the top of a cage. There was a curtain that
was supposed to be covering it, but it had been pulled to the side.
The room looked very dark and very dirty inside.

Tim had to admit it was really interesting. When they got back to the
classroom, everyone would be dying to hear them tell the story
again. Especially, Tim hoped, Erica.

They crept a little closer to the window and leaned out from behind
the trash can they were hiding behind. Tim frowned. He leaned

closer still, and saw something that made his stomach drop and his heart beat faster.

There was a hand inside the cage. A human hand.

It was holding on to the top of the cage, the fingers curled around the bars of the cage. The fingers were dirty… and the nails had a tinge of red on them.

"Do you see that, Tim?" asked Derrick.

"Yes," Tim whispered. He didn't mean to whisper. He didn't even realize he whispered. He was watching that hand with all of his concentration.

It moved a little. Grasped the bars tighter, the nails turning white with the effort.

Both boys looked at the hand, looked horrified, looked at each other. They tried to turn away and head back to school, starting to realize that they were going to be missed soon.

But they couldn't stop looking at the hand. They were mystified, their primordial morbid curiosity growing with each second.

"We really need to go now," said Derrick.

"Yeah," Tim whispered.

They both started to turn away when a face suddenly appeared in the window, looked the boys right in the eyes, and then disappeared. The curtain was pulled abruptly back into place. And the door by the window burst open.

The face from the window, attached to a very large scary body, was coming toward them very fast.

The boys both yelled and turned to run.

It was too late. Two impossibly strong hands caught them by their arms and drug them back toward the door faster than they thought was humanly possible.

They were right. It wasn't humanly possible.

They were drug into the darkness inside and the door slammed closed.

THE END

Sneak Peek of Book Three:

Tim and Derrick were in adjoining cages. They had both been crying, and were now in that stage after crying, probably shock. They were both just staring at the bottom of their cages.

They had both started to scream, but the dirty man that dragged them into the room had beaten them, then tied rags around their mouths and tied their hands behind their backs, shoving them into their cages roughly.

They looked around the room and everything they saw made them more terrified. There were probably two dozen cages in the room. There were two rusty doors, one leading outside, which they'd been brought through, and one leading deeper into the building. There was a light fixture hanging from the ceiling with a broken light bulb in the socket. There was a chair in the middle of the room, and a tray next to it with rusty metal things lying on it. They looked like tools or instruments of some kind. They looked scary.

The big, dirty man who had brought them in, after beating them and tying them up, had gone through the other door, deeper into the building. They heard noises from behind that door, and hoped they never went there. Strange thumps and muffled screams and awful laughing came from behind that door.

Tim and Derrick looked into the other cages in their room and saw seven other people. Four were kids like them, two were women, and one was an old man. They had all clearly been beaten and were tied up with rags in their mouths. They were all dirty, and from the streaks on their faces had all been crying.

One of the kids was in a cage close to Tim's. She looked like she was about six years old. She tossed a note into Tim's cage. Tim moved around to pick it up, but it was hard to do with his hands tied. He turned around and was just about to grab it when the door opened. He sat down on the note.

The dirty man came in and looked around the room at the cages. He was thin, not very tall now that Tim had a chance to really look at him. He was kind of gangly in a nerd kind of way. He was wearing brown pants and a short sleeve collared shirt that looked like it was missing its pocket protector. He was bald on top and had longish hair on the sides which was wet and dripping onto his shoulders. He wore thick glasses and muttered to himself. "They never found her body…" he mumbled. He smiled a very ugly smile, went to the cage where the six-year-old girl was, opened it, and dragged her out. She tried to cry out, tried to fight against him, but he hit her hard and she fell to the ground, stunned and almost blacked out.

He picked her up and carried her through the door and deeper into the building. The door slammed shut.

Tim rolled over, picked up the note in his hands, and unfolded it, laying it flat. He turned around and saw it was upside down with the print against the floor. With an impatient noise, he turned back around, flipped the note over, and turned back.

The note said, "Whatever you do, don't let them take you through that door".

Made in the USA
Lexington, KY
29 November 2019